"THERE IT IS, OFFICER!"

St. Bede's processional crucifix was lying on top of a display case in plain view, quite near the doors. Belle-Mère's chalice was there, too, together with a number of other things that Mother Grey wouldn't have thought it worthwhile to steal, including her black vestments. Satanists! Pillaging her church!

Suddenly she saw protruding from behind the glass display case a pair of feet, toes down, encased in shoes with perfectly featureless soles, maybe a man's size nine. They were different from the shoes that had tramped mud all over her church, bigger, more rounded in the toes. But the important thing about them was, there were feet in them.

She put her hands to her head. "I don't want to do this anymore," she muttered.

"What?" said Officer Kreevitch.

"I want you to look behind that case and tell me it isn't a body."

He looked, turned pale, and cursed.

Also by Kate Gallison

BURY THE BISHOP

DEVIL'S WORKSHOP

#2

Kate Gallison

A DELL BOOK

Published by
Dell Publishing
a division of
Bantam Doubleday Dell Publishing Group, Inc.
1540 Broadway
New York, New York 10036

ISBN: 0-440-22219-2

Printed in the United States of America

Published simultaneously in Canada

February 1996

10 9 8 7 6 5 4 3 2 1

RAD

To the gang at St. Andrew's,
good sports all

1

It was a shame about the weather. If not for the continuously pounding sleet, today would have been perfect for Celia Warthen's wedding.

Mother Grey had buried a number of people since she became the vicar of St. Bede's, and baptized two, but this was her first wedding. She was all keyed up and ready for the experience. Perhaps it was this and not the sound of ice on the rectory windows that had given her such a restless night, nightmares about cats, wakefulness in the small hours. She peered through her bedroom window and saw that a glassy coating covered the whole town of Fishersville, the bushes and trees, the electric wires, her Chevy Nova, everything, to a depth of half an inch. This would be a problem for the wedding guests. She fed Towser and took him out for his walk; the two of them went almost a block and then by mutual consent turned around and came home again.

While Mother Grey's oatmeal was cooking, the phone rang. It was Ellen Warthen, calling to reassure her about daughter Celia's wedding. In spite of the severity of the weather, she said, they were going ahead as planned, one o'clock at St. Bede's.

"Most of the out-of-town guests are here already," Mrs. Warthen said. "Fortunately." No sooner had Mother Grey hung up the phone than the florist and her assistant appeared at the rectory door, wanting the key to the church.

Soon there would be rich people traipsing up and down the church steps, some of them North Jersey lawyers. When Mother Grey finished her breakfast, she took her trusty coal shovel and bucket of salt and went out to inspect the walkways for ice. This liability patrol was becoming a routine with her. St. Bede's at this point in its life could ill afford to be sued. The parish had come a long way in the three years since Mother Grey first came here to be vicar, but for all that she had accomplished in growth of the parish and service to the surrounding community, the church was still broke. Furthermore, Mother Grey had a powerful enemy serving in the Diocesan Department of Missions, namely Father Rupert Bingley. She could just hear him: "A lawsuit, Mother Grey?

This won't do at all. You'll have to close St. Bede's now."

So far this winter, no one had fallen down on church property, though people were dropping like flies all over town. Everyone agreed it was one of the worst winters in Fishersville history. Not only did it storm two and three times a week, so that schools all over New Jersey had to be closed and travel became all but impossible, but there was also the thing with the cats.

No one knew what happened to them. Some said they wandered off and froze to death in the storms, but their dead bodies were never seen. Mother Grey herself had no cats. She had Towser, the peebie-jeevie who had come into her life two years before in a wounded condition and made himself her dog. Having no cats, she felt sympathy when the lost-cat handbills began appearing, some with photos, others in childish scrawls, on phone poles all over Fishersville, but she did not feel menaced. Still, she couldn't help wondering what was behind it.

It was strange. Cat owners began to keep their animals indoors. The police did nothing because they could think of nothing to do and because, like everyone else in Fishersville, they were too busy trying to survive the winter to worry about cats.

When Mother Grey appeared at the church with her salt and her shovel, movers were unloading a rented harpsichord. She got busy chipping and salting. As she finished clearing the bottom

step, the florist came out the front door, followed
by her assistant, and gave her back the key.

She went inside to take a look. They had be-
decked the inside of the old stone church with
more white flowers than Mother Grey could ever
remember having seen in one place. For a moment the storm clouds parted and let the sunlight
through the stained-glass windows, and the beautiful saints and angels seemed to smile on the
oaken pews with their flowers and ribbons. St.
Bede's had never looked lovelier. *Mine,* said a
small voice in Mother Grey's head.

Hers by the grace of God and the skin of her
teeth. Since her arrival here as vicar, the congregation at St. Bede's had perhaps quadrupled (not
difficult; she had started with five people). The diocesan assessment had been paid every year, although Mother Grey had had to forgo ten
thousand dollars in back pay to do it. Slow im-
provements had been made to the dilapidated
church, mostly things that Mother Grey and her
parishioners were able to do with their own
hands—the painting of the porches and window
frames, the refinishing of the pews. Her parishioners were few but wonderful people. The Warthens had money, the Wellworths had intelligence
and charm, Delight van Buskirk had, at age
ninety-four, venerability, and Saraleigh and
Ralph—well, they were poor, stupid, charmless,
and young, but they had loyal hearts and willing
hands.

Mother Grey still remembered with shame

and rage the day when Father Rupert Bingley had presented his bald fat self at her door and proposed to merge St. Bede's with his own prosperous parish, ten minutes by car from Fishersville, and carry her entire congregation away in a minibus to attend St. Dinarius. If she prayed about it enough, she might someday be able to forgive him.

Forgiving him would be easier if he stopped pressing his offensive proposal. Now that Bingley was in the Diocesan Department of Missions, under canon law he had power over St. Bede's as a mission church. When he came to the parish on business, she often caught him gazing on St. Bede's stained-glass windows with a covetous eye.

It was touch and go with Bingley. Everything that happened at St. Bede's became an occasion for him to come around and try to close the church. Right after Christmas, St. Bede's furnace gave up the ghost. Throughout the month of January, she burned incense every Sunday because the smell of something burning seemed to give the worshipers the illusion that they were warm. Sometimes Ralph Voercker, her corpulent thirty-two-year-old acolyte, tried to do fancy things with it like swinging the censer around in a circle by the chain, but he lacked the necessary coordination. At other times he would surreptitiously warm his hands on it until she feared that he would set the flowing white sleeves of his cotta on fire.

Fortunately Major and Mrs. Warthen gave Mother Grey the money for a new furnace just before Bingley's last visit, so that she was able to wave the check at him when he complained that you couldn't run a church without heat. Lucky for St. Bede's that Major and Mrs. Warthen had money.

But enough of brooding over the outrages of Bingley. It was time to see about the vestments. Edward Warthen was to serve as an acolyte at his sister's wedding, and Mother Grey needed to be sure his cassock and cotta were pressed. She went to the sacristy and checked out all the necessary vestments, her own as well, shaking and brushing them, running over the cotta with a warm iron, being careful not to scorch it. These things would not fit him next year. At thirteen, Edward was undoubtedly on the brink of a growth spurt. Soon he would be taller than Mother Grey herself.

Three years at St. Bede's, and this was her first wedding. Next week, another wedding: Ralph and Saraleigh. High time for those two. Ralph had been working in the mail room of the paper-bag factory for six months, eligible at last for health benefits for himself and his dependents, if any. This meant that Saraleigh could afford to get off welfare, drop the Medicaid coverage for her three children, and marry him at last. With luck some of these flowers would still be blooming at their wedding.

Everything was in readiness. A shame about the weather. But then, life in Fishersville was such that a natural disaster (for that was what they were now beginning to call the snow) only enhanced its charms. Mother Grey stood on the porch of St. Bede's and beamed with pleasure on the neighbors digging one another's cars out, on the yuppies cross-country skiing, on the city officials who turned out to supervise or even personally engage in snow removal. She fell into a meditation on the order and beauty of life in Fishersville, little knowing the extent of the disorder underneath, little guessing how it was about to erupt.

"When can I get a bus to Fishersville?"

The boy behind the lunch counter looked up at Rex Perskie and took his time answering. Perskie was not happy to be in Trenton. The minute he got off the bus from Jacksonville, Florida, and stepped into the Trenton winter, Perskie realized he had forgotten how unpleasant New Jersey could be in February. Maybe he should have stayed in Florida after he got out.

There was so little demand for buses from Trenton to Fishersville that the boy had to look at a schedule folded up beside the cash register. "Five o'clock," he said finally.

"What? Lemme see that thing." Perskie snatched it from his hand.

"Keep it," said the kid. "They're free."

Five o'clock? Spend a whole afternoon in Trenton? The kid must have read it wrong. Perskie could walk to Fishersville and be there before three—hell, he could run it. Couldn't be more than twenty miles. He had grown very fit in prison, put on thirty pounds of muscle. He imagined himself jogging up the river, taking the canal path maybe. The wet gravel crunching under his feet. Roll in about suppertime, sneak into the old place, give Saraleigh a thrill. His woman. Family life. This time he would straighten her out a little better than last time.

If the old place was still there. He sort of remembered it being on fire when he left.

Trenton to Fishersville. Here it was. Five o'clock was when the next bus came, the only bus. He could find a bar, kill three or four hours in Trenton, or he could walk. Or try to hitch a ride. As if anyone would pick him up, with his prison haircut and his ex-con shirt and pants.

"Do you know if there's a clothing store around here somewhere?" he asked the kid.

"Sporting goods store about four blocks up State Street," the kid said. "They might have a hat and a warm jacket. You from Florida?"

"I'm from Fishersville," said Perskie. "And now I'm going back there."

2

The place where Celia Warthen chose to hold her wedding reception was not the Fishers Arms Hotel (it was booked for many months ahead; the couple had not wanted a long engagement), nor the old Wagonner mansion on Ash Street where the Warthens were living (the caterer pronounced even that huge house too small for the desired number of guests), nor yet the rescue squad hall (it lacked the required cachet). She held her reception in the Umbrella Works.

The Umbrella Works was not a hotel or restaurant but a kind of architectural antiques store. It had once been a factory. The main floor formed a large airy space, good for big gatherings. A number of wedding receptions had been held there, although all of them were weddings of newcomers to the town, and none included families whose members had ever been employed there when the factory was producing umbrellas.

Nothing in Fishersville was more typical of the town's recent changes than the Umbrella Works. From a greasy little river town with a few dying factories, Fishersville had somehow become a picturesque hot spot for tourists from New York. Every temperate weekend, these people jammed the main street, parking their BMWs and Jaguars in front of hydrants and in spaces better deserved by honest taxpayers (it was said by the locals), neglecting to put quarters in the meters, howling with rage when Chief Harry had their cars ticketed. Of all the normal places where the locals used to shop, only the Acme, the hardware store, and Delio's luncheonette had survived the rolling tide of chic.

Delio's, where you could get a cup of real coffee without gourmet admixtures and an unapologetically greasy doughnut, was the last retreat of the locals from the fern-bar atmosphere that the tourists seemed somehow to have brought with them to the other eateries in town. Mother Grey herself ate breakfast there three times a week and got an earful from the locals about the way the town was going. The storefronts that once purveyed such useful items as hardware, musical instruments, baked goods, and shoes were now occupied by antique dealers, their windows exhibiting worn rugs, obsolete household utensils, rickety furniture, and crazed china, artfully arranged with swags of chintz. Junk shops, said the locals.

Only last week the *Clarion* ran a story about the proprietors of some of these establishments: how they were beginning to demand privileges from the city government, parking concessions and the like, on the grounds that they had saved the town from working-class mediocrity and made it what it was today. The article was the talk of Delio's for days.

Of all the junk shops, the Umbrella Works (née Wagonner Brothers Manufacturing) was the biggest and fanciest. Simon Ratcher, a rich dealer from New York, had created it out of the defunct umbrella factory like a Frankenstein's monster out of dead body parts.

First he had hired out-of-town architects to embellish the place, and when the architects got finished, it looked more like an old factory than ever, except that you couldn't get work there. Where the railroad tracks used to be, between the factory and the river, he put a flagstone patio. Then he installed a walk-in fireplace. Finally he replaced the old broken neon sign on the roof with a new sign, hand-carved, UMBRELLA WORKS in gold lettering with no neon. (Tourists liked neon only when the intention was clearly camp.) The cavernous space inside housed art, used furniture, linens, china, old toys, and Ratcher's specialty, "architectural antiques," things torn from demolished buildings in deteriorating East Coast cities. Piles of worm-eaten paneling, disembodied columns, fireplace surrounds without any hearth, ornate stairways to nowhere—all were for sale, all were arranged in excruciatingly artful compositions.

This particular junk shop had so much style and panache that the Umbrella Works became an overnight success, a mecca for collectors from all over the East Coast. Bruce Springsteen had been seen shopping there. The most fashionable brides in central Jersey wanted it for their receptions; it provided a most romantic background for the wedding video.

Mother Grey looked around at the astonishing decor when she had finished shaking hands and murmuring platitudes in Celia Warthen's reception line. This was the first time she had been inside the famous Umbrella Works. The same florist who had embellished the church had done the decorations for the reception, airy draperies of pastel chiffon swagged from staircase to pillar and anchored with sprays of freesia. On a balcony salvaged from a ruined building, a string quartet played softly (and rather too sluggishly for Mother Grey's taste, but this was not after all a musical event). Small dining tables draped with lace were arranged in clusters between and around the architectural elements, giving the gathering of several hundred people a surprisingly intimate air. The buffet of food was beautifully arranged; the guests were gorgeously dressed. It was like a movie set.

Mother Grey found a place by herself at a little

table near the fire, underneath the torpid musicians, and began to nibble. It was good to sit down. The Warthens seemed to have invited nobody she knew, except for Ellen Warthen's brother, Rodman Sedgewick, and his wife, Ouida, both of them bores, and their two burly sons, Chip and Lance. Rodman and Ouida Sedgewick attended church at St. Dinarius, the church where Mother Grey's bête noire, Rupert Bingley, was rector. Rodman Sedgewick stood on the other side of the huge room, a glass of what was probably Scotch in his professionally manicured hand, braying at some luckless soul foolish enough to have solicited his opinions about medical insurance while standing backed into a corner. Mother Grey could hear his voice clearly over the murmured voices of the other guests. Someone had mentioned that he was planning to run for the Senate. In another corner Chip and Lance were hitting on the bridesmaids.

Mother Grey was moved to ask herself why, in the midst of all this revelry, she wasn't having any fun. It must be that she was tired. Between her struggles with the weather and getting the church just right, and then worrying about the ceremony itself, she had worn herself out completely. The food, catered by the best restaurateur in town, was delicious. The wine, rather than taking the edge off her natural shyness, filled her with languor, as did the warmth from Ratcher's big fireplace, so that she felt more and more distant from all that was going on around her. She would have liked to go home and sleep.

She missed Dave Dogg.

Dave had gone to Boston for the funeral of his ex-wife's mother. A noble deed, but it made Mother Grey uneasy. For one thing, he had been away for almost a week now; how long could it take to bury one old lady? What was he doing? Mother Grey had her suspicions, actually. She had noticed Felicia Dogg leaning on Dave more and more, pulling at him with her personal concerns beyond the concerns they shared for their son. Lately on Saturday evenings, Felicia had taken to calling and asking for Dave at the rectory. After the third incident of this sort, Mother Grey began to conclude that Dave's ex-wife wanted him back. She was torn between the urge to fight for him and the pious desire to honor the sanctity of the marital tie. Anyway, how did one fight for a man? She wouldn't know how to begin. New lipstick, maybe. Victoria's Secret underwear. Wrestling and hair-pulling matches with Felicia, out behind the soda shop, the way the girls she went to high school with used to do.

I wish these musicians would pick up the tempo, she thought. What she needed was to make some music herself. It was high time she got another violoncello to replace Granny's Weaver that had burned up in the rectory fire. A year and a half without an instrument had surely caused all her skills to atrophy. But good cellos were so expensive.

Ellen Warthen, delicately beautiful in peacock moiré taffeta, appeared from behind a staircase and sat down with a rustle at the little table across from her. "Mother Vinnie!" she said. "You look so pensive."

The Warthens had moved to town the previous summer. When they began attending St. Bede's, Mother Grey was jubilant. Besides swelling the ranks by four new members, themselves and the two children, they raised the general tone of the congregation. Unlike some of her flock (Ralph and Saraleigh for example), Major and Mrs. Warthen were cultured people; they read; they enjoyed classical music. Ellen Warthen was a gifted watercolorist. It wasn't so much that Mother Grey was snobbish, she told herself, but that she felt lonely sometimes for people who shared her tastes and interests.

"I guess I'm too tired to decently enjoy a party," she said to Ellen Warthen. "You look wonderful. How do you do it?" Ellen Warthen laughed, her charming little laugh that ran up the scale. Mother Grey had always thought of her as fragile, like a bone china teacup that you could see your fingers through if you held it up to the light. Yet she seemed to have everything in hand, the whirlwind wedding, the care of a husband and teenage boy, even her personal grooming, which was enviable, not a hair out of place. She looked rested, vibrant. Now here she was finding time to be a gracious hostess to Mother Grey, moping in her corner.

"Celia and I went to New York yesterday to have our hair done," she said.

No, that isn't it, thought Mother Grey. *There's something else.* Ellen Warthen's radiance was something beyond what could be conferred by even the most skilled New York hairdresser. She might have been the bride herself. She gave a happy sigh and wiggled her shoulders. "I'm so glad we could do this wedding here in Fishersville," she said, "instead of overseas somewhere. I love it here. We want to buy the house we're living in, if old Mr. Wagonner will sell it to us."

"Small-town life can be very satisfying," said Mother Grey.

"I'm going to turn the garage into my painting studio," she said. "It's heated. Did you know that? When we own it, we can put in a north skylight." Was this the source of Ellen's glow, the joy of art? A heated garage, or any sort of garage, was a rare thing in Fishersville. "We've never owned our own home, you know, in all the years we've been married. My brother Roddy's country place, where he and I grew up, is the closest thing I know to a permanent home."

"I thought your family lived in Washington when you were a child."

"That was Uncle Bertie. He was a senator for two terms. Daddy was more of a power behind the throne, so we stayed on the farm in New Jersey." The farm, Mother Grey recalled, was more like a feudal holding, acre after acre of pastureland spanning two counties in the central Jersey horse country. She had been there once. The pillared farmhouse overlooked a real racetrack.

"So after you were married, you and Armstrong led the nomadic military life," said Mother Grey. "How many countries have you lived in?"

"Six. Seven. I've lost count. Now and then we were posted to Washington in between times."

"Is the major back in the States to stay?"

"He's virtually retired," she said. "The job at Princeton is just to keep him busy. But why are you sitting all by yourself with a long face? Come and meet the guests."

"I was thinking how much I miss my cello."

"I never knew you played the cello. What happened to it?"

"I lost it in the rectory fire."

"Ah." The rectory fire was a mythic occurrence in Fishersville. Even the Warthens had heard of it, though it had happened before they moved to town. "You'll have to get another. Maybe Simon Ratcher has one here in his shop. I think he carries a few musical instruments; let's ask him. Perhaps he'll give you a break on the price."

"Maybe he has another Weaver for me." Another Weaver. One could always hope. If Mother Grey ever encountered such a thing, she wouldn't be able to afford it. The Weaver had been a wedding present from her grandmother to her mother, a priceless treasure made by the finest luthier in Washington out of an old door to the White House removed in the renovations during the Truman administration.

17

After the Weaver burned, she could never bring herself to replace it with an inferior instrument. She knew it was stupid, but she really didn't have the money, and with the cares of the parish, she really didn't have the time to search for a new cello.

"There's Simon now," said Ellen Warthen. She pointed across the room to the doors to the sculpture garden, where Ratcher was coming in carrying firewood, surrounded by a group of handsome youths. The antique dealer had made a concession to the formal nature of the occasion by donning a vintage smoking jacket over his customary turtleneck and baggy pants. The jacket, paisley silk in a deep burgundy color, had a collar and cuffs of quilted black velvet. A little extra brilliantine on the thinning hair slicked into his usual ponytail completed the effect, more that of a pudgy Sherlock Holmes in his boudoir than of a correctly dressed guest at a wedding.

When his gaze met Ellen Warthen's, he excused himself to the boys, dropped the wood by the fireplace, and came across the room to her. This was the first time Mother Grey had experienced Ratcher up close, although like everyone else, she had seen him around town, strutting along Main Street, discoursing with the other dealers or purchasing coffee and a muffin at Delio's, where he never stopped to eat with the locals. He wore scent—sandalwood and patchouli.

"Darling," he purred, still holding Ellen Warthen's gaze. "I found the most exquisite eighteenth-century cherry armoire for you. Say the word and it's yours." He took her hand and pressed it to his lips. "You look divine," he murmured. Mother Grey thought it was the greasiest exhibition she had ever witnessed. Is this how they were selling used furniture nowadays? Ellen Warthen blushed and dropped her eyes as though he had engaged her feelings somehow. Well. There was no accounting for some people's taste in men. The slimy New Age Simon Ratcher couldn't be more unlike Ellen Warthen's husband. Major Warthen was an old-school preppy type; Dave referred to him as a rich stiff.

"Won't you introduce me?" Ratcher said, turning his eyes to Mother Grey. They were really startling eyes, green with dark brows and lashes. Perhaps it was the green eyes that flustered Ellen Warthen. Still, Mother Grey could not have called the man attractive.

Ellen Warthen pulled herself together and made introductions. "Lavinia Grey, may I present Simon Ratcher. Simon, Mother Grey needs an inexpensive cello. I told her you might have one here somewhere."

The hand he placed in hers felt warm, dry, oddly rough for a man who seemed so creamed and perfumed. *He must do all his own furniture moving,* she thought.

He smiled. "A cello? No, I don't have one. But if you'd like me to, I can keep an eye out for such an item."

"Thank you," she said.

"What did you want to spend?"

"Three, maybe four hundred dollars."

His lips twisted into an expression somewhere between scorn and pity.

As a pall of social discomfort settled over Mother Grey and her two companions, suddenly the bride appeared, exquisitely beautiful in a confection of creamy lace and pearls. Celia Warthen looked very like her mother. They both had the same color eyes, the blue of wild chicory blossoms, the same heart-shaped faces, the same fair skin lightly sprinkled with freckles, the same hair.

New York hair, mused Mother Grey. Maybe that was what she needed in the war for Dave Dogg. A New York hairdresser.

"Mother, come on! We're cutting the cake!" The bride and her mother went off in the direction of the wedding cake, where it towered over a lace and chiffon-draped table. Mother Grey got up to follow them. She felt Simon Ratcher's hand on her shoulder. "Can we talk for a moment?" he said. "There's something I've been wanting to ask you, Mother Grey."

"Yes?" She couldn't imagine what it might be.

"I hear you have a nineteenth-century brass processional crucifix at St. Bede's in fairly good condition."

"We're pleased with it," said Mother Grey. "It adds a certain tone to the liturgy."

"I have a buyer for it."

"Have you."

"This person is a very wealthy collector. He

needs this piece to fill out his collection. Just for that reason, and not because it's actually worth that much, I'm prepared to offer you five thousand dollars."

"It belongs to the church, Mr. Ratcher. Even if I wanted to, I couldn't let you have it on my own authority. The Diocesan Department of Missions has charge of the business affairs of St. Bede's, you know. We are a mission church."

"Surely you can't believe anyone in the Diocese of New Jersey would actually notice that St. Bede's processional crucifix was gone."

Would anyone in the diocese notice? Probably not. Indeed, at times Mother Grey felt that no one in the Diocese of New Jersey would notice if St. Bede's in its entirety were to fall through a hole in the earth. (Excepting Rupert Bingley, who would want the stained-glass windows and the walnut pulpit for his own parish church, together with Mother Grey's parishioners, and after that a grandstand seat where he could watch while St. Bede's fell in the hole.)

It was no less an authority than the late Bishop Wealle who had given Mother Grey as her first assignment as a priest the task of gracefully closing up the failing church. By stubbornly keeping it open, she had caused the powers in Trenton to turn their faces from her. Now and then Bingley came around from the Department of Missions to check on whether St. Bede's was dead yet, but as far as she knew, he hadn't actually taken inventory

of the equipment. (Or had he noticed the crucifix?)

None of this, of course, was any of Simon
Ratcher's business. "Perhaps you're right. Still, I
must decline your offer, thank you very much."

"Think about it. I could make it six thousand.
You can buy a middling-good cello for six thousand fish."

"I'm afraid it's out of the question."

The antique dealer smiled, nodded, and
moved away toward the cake-cutting ceremony.
Mother Grey had the sensation of having encountered an arty Beelzebub in a smoking jacket. And
yet, why not sell the crucifix? Think of the money.
Of course she could never put it to personal use—
that would be criminal as well as immoral. But
for the church and the community. In two weeks
St. Bede's new day-care center was supposed to
open. The inspectors were bound to find many expensive deficiencies on their visit Tuesday.

Simon Ratcher was right about one thing.
With the possible exception of Father Bingley, no
one in the diocese would ever miss the crucifix,
not for years, perhaps not in her lifetime. But that
wouldn't make it right to let St. Bede's processional crucifix go for mere money.

And if Bingley were to discover that she was
selling off the church furnishings—!

Desperate for distraction from this line of
thought, Mother Grey cast her eyes around the
surreal environment for a familiar face. When at
last she saw one, it was, alas, the face of Rodman

Sedgewick. He smiled and came charging toward her.

The bride's uncle Rodman was known to Mother Grey because he gave things to her. Somehow the Sedgewicks had fixed on St. Bede's as the most worthy recipient for the things they wanted to give away. Their gifts were never as useful as other things might have been—for example, money. Since Mr. and Mrs. Sedgewick were his parishioners, Mother Grey suspected Father Bingley himself of directing the largess of the Sedgewicks her way; she could hear him now: "Oh, Mr. Sedgewick, these gifts would do so much more good at St. Bede's. A poor mission church, you know. Dear Mother Grey works so hard."

The gift of the month before had been seven obsolete desktop computers, cast off by Sedgewick's law firm when the partners replaced them with the latest and hottest. They had no hard drives and only 64K of RAM (whatever that was), so no one answered the ad she ran in the paper. Mother Grey doubted whether even Simon Ratcher himself could have made the old computers look good, although someone had mentioned to her that they were becoming collectible.

Four of these electronic gifts were still piled in the back of the church. One she had installed in her office, against the time when she or Saraleigh figured out how to use it. Two others her chief acolyte and vestryman Ralph Voercker had carried away to the old group home where he used to live before he decided he was sane. Maybe the other disturbed young men could teach themselves to do something with them and so find useful careers at last.

Most of the young men in the group home were coming along nicely. Only a year ago (it seemed like a hundred), Mother Grey herself had rescued the young men's halfway house at 14 Main Street when the Mental Health Foundation had been ready to abandon the group home project for lack of funding. Of course, her efforts in that cause had not been entirely altruistic. The halfway house was where Ralph Voercker went whenever he had a fight with Saraleigh. If the halfway house hadn't been there for him, he would have come to the rectory to live, and Saraleigh would have come after him, bringing her cigarettes and her crying babies, making ugly scenes on the rectory steps, holding loud tearful late-night reconciliations in the backyard. Thanks be to God, these episodes were becoming less and less frequent.

Mother Grey's self-interest in the group home project never became apparent to the state agency that finally gave her the grant for the group home. That was because Ralph was not related to her by blood, though he had been her particular charge ever since the night two years before, when she saved him from throwing himself over the wing dam. If she had actually been his mother instead of a mere mother-figure, the state would most likely have declared a conflict of interest on her part and denied her the grant money.

That would have been a shame. The home would have had to close. All the disturbed young men would have had to leave Fishersville and go live in places where they could afford the rent on their SSI stipends. As it was, they were all doing so well, with their steady (if ill-paying) jobs at places like the paper-bag factory and their nourishing social networks. There was so much more trouble to get into in places like Trenton.

Ralph, at least, was making a success of his own employment in the mail room of the paperbag factory. Friday would mark the end of his sixmonth probation period on the job; he would have health insurance coverage. Saturday he and Saraleigh were to be married. It might be that computer skills had something to do with it; you never knew.

So here came Rodman Sedgewick. "Mother Vinnie!" he said in his heartiest politician's voice, shaking her hand and clapping her on the shoulder. It was like being accosted by a well-groomed bear. His physical presence was imposing, as became a senatorial candidate; he was tall and solid, with a big chin, and his hands were the hard hands of a horseman. "How are you enjoying the reception? Can we get you anything more to eat or drink?"

"Thank you, no," she said. "How are you, Rodman? I keep hearing rumors about your political career. Is it true that you'll be on the ballot in the next primary?"

"I am planning to offer my services to the electorate," he said. "You have heard correctly. Someone needs to carry the banner of the flat tax to the people."

"What's the flat tax?" she said. Right away, she could have torn out her tongue for asking. Sedgewick filled his chest with air and began to rant about his economic plan, which as near as Mother Grey could determine involved huge tax cuts for the rich and the elimination of all government social programs.

"That would be very hard on the day-care center we're trying to open at St. Bede's," she said when at last he stopped to draw a breath. "We're going to need public funding."

"Under my plan such programs would be funded by the private sector," said Rodman Sedgewick.

"Then perhaps I can count on you for a contribution."

His face lit up. "Indeed you can," he said. "In fact, I have just the thing for your new day-care center."

"Some money?"

"No, more of an in-kind contribution. We'll keep it as a surprise till tomorrow," he said.

Then his wife, Ouida, rushed up and seized him by the arm, as she so often seemed to do when Sedgewick was talking to other women. "Isn't this the loveliest wedding, Mother Grey?" she said. "Roddy, Arthur Snell is here. He wants to talk to you about the campaign." They excused themselves and dived into the crowd.

So. Another gift. Mother Grey couldn't imagine what Sedgewick was going to give her this time. She didn't want to imagine. Sufficient unto the day is the evil thereof.

There was a hubbub on one of the staircases; the bride appeared to be flinging her garter. Soon it would be time to go home to the rectory and give Towser his treat. In the pocket of her good suit, Mother Grey had squirreled away four liver paté canapés, wrapped in a cocktail napkin that said CELIA AND ANTHONY in gold ink.

There would be nothing as fancy as napkins saying SARALEIGH AND RALPH next week. Mother Grey would perform their ceremony also. The happy couple would not be having their reception at the Umbrella Works or even the firehouse, but Mother Grey and some of the parishioners were planning a little party in the rectory. There would be a cake, made by ninety-four-year-old Delight van Buskirk, and great rejoicing in the parish. Freddy Kane, Saraleigh's eldest, was to be ring bearer; Martine Wellworth, another of the treasures of Mother Grey's flock, had taken him to the mall and bought him a suit, to his intense mortification. Nine-year-olds did not enjoy dressing up.

A cheer went up; the bride and groom were leaving. Mother Grey took one last look around the fairyland that was the Umbrella Works, took one last good lungful of freesia, furniture wax, and expensive perfume, and began heading for her coat.

Her way led through the crowd and around

various of the large and small *objets* of Simon Ratcher's collection. Behind a disembodied staircase she was surprised to see bookshelves. Evidently Simon Ratcher sold old books, some of them appearing to be rare, leather-bound or bound in waxy yellowish stuff. *I'll just have a look at these,* she thought, *and then I'll get my coat and make my good-byes.*

As she examined the books, she became aware of two small figures sitting quietly in the shadows at the foot of the staircase. It was Edward Warthen, with his halo of yellow curls, and a bigger boy, a pale unhealthy-looking child whose dark hair fell straight and greasy over his eyes. The two heads were bent over a small black book. Mother Grey could see part of the title, *Grim* something; yellow Post-It notes protruded from between the book's worn pages.

Another Post-It was lying on the floor at her feet, as though it had fallen out. She picked it up. There were words written on the slip in block letters, but she couldn't understand them; they seemed to be in a foreign language she had never studied. "Aglon," she murmured. "Tetragram . . . Vaycheon . . ."

The boys looked up at her suddenly. The dark-haired boy snickered. Edward said, "Don't say those words out loud, Mother Grey." His thin face was very serious, intense, and scholarly. He had wild-chicory eyes like his sister's.

"Why not?" she said.

"You haven't drawn the circle." He reached out and took the slip of paper from her hand.

"Circle?" But the two boys had melted into the crowd of merrymakers, taking the book with them.

The implications of this scene had scarcely begun to gnaw at the edges of her mind when she bumped into her host, enjoying a moment of solitude behind some potted palms. She extended her hand to him, hoping to make her good-byes. Too late, she realized that the major was somewhat the worse for the Rob Roys. Before she realized what he was doing, he pulled her forward and planted an extremely erotic kiss on the side of her neck.

"You know, you're a very attractive woman," he murmured.

Yes, I do know that. But I'm not here in that capacity. "A wonderful party," she said. "Excuse me." She disengaged herself and rushed for the coat racks, screaming inwardly: *Enough! Enough!* This was all the entertainment Mother Grey could stand in one session.

3

The cold air outside was refreshing. As she picked her way home over the icy sidewalks, Mother Grey looked up to see a rough-looking man, collar up, black knitted hat pulled down, standing in the street with his face turned toward the east wall of St. Bede's. Although she couldn't see his features, something about the man's appearance was familiar. Was it one of her AA members from years ago? Why was he staring at the church that way?

She was almost close enough to have a good look at him when the man turned away and went down High Street in the direction of the lot where the old rectory had been. An oddly aggressive walk, almost a swagger. She watched him turn the corner and disappear.

I know him, she thought. *Who is he?*

High Street was all different from the way it had been when Rex Perskie left. The apartment house where he had lived with Saraleigh had been replaced with two modest brick row houses with garages underneath them. Could she still be there, living in one of the houses? Could you live in a house and be on welfare? There was a Mercedes-Benz parked out front of one of the garages. Money. That wouldn't be Saraleigh's neighborhood anymore.

After the fire she had taken the kids across the street, right? To the reverend's house. But, hey, it wasn't there. Nothing there but a vacant lot now. She must be someplace. Saraleigh would never leave town.

Perskie's feet were hurting from the cold. As long as he was hiking at a good pace, he didn't feel it, even though his shoes and socks were wet through, but now he was in pain. The hat and coat he had picked up at the army surplus store were good, but they weren't enough. He had to get in out of this. He would go to City Hall, see his old pals in the police station. Maybe they hadn't heard he was in the tank. Maybe they would give him a job. At least they'd let him sit by the radiator for five minutes.

As Perskie approached City Hall, the fire horn

went off with a loud blast that startled him. He had forgotten how noisy the town was, the fire horn, the rescue squad siren. You think of it as a quiet place.

The fire horn. He could almost remember what had happened before he went to Florida and got in trouble. The fire horn. Something was on fire. Jesus, it was him. No, it was his furniture. He was on the sofa. It was burning.

After that, he tried to get Saraleigh to bring the kids and live in his car up on Reeker's Hill. She wouldn't do it. Did she dump him? Could that bitch have dumped him? He had tried to write her from jail, but the letters were returned, No Forwarding Address. She was here in Fishersville someplace, though, or somewhere in the county anyway. If she left the county, she'd lose her welfare checks. He knew she would never go out and work.

Perskie glanced down toward the river and was surprised to see signs of life in the old umbrella factory, the last place he had held a steady job. Somebody had painted it and fixed the windows. The old neon sign, POP-O UMBRELLAS, was gone. In its place was a new wooden one with the letters carved out and painted gold: UMBRELLA WORKS. The factory was open. The lights were on. Maybe they were hiring. He went to check it out.

Mother Grey threw some more rock salt onto the front steps and let herself into the rectory. The

whole house smelled of fresh coffee. Deacon Deedee Gilchrist must have arrived.

Deedee, Mother Grey's old roommate from
seminary, came to visit sometimes, less often now
that Mother Grey was seeing so much of Dave
Dogg. Not that Deedee didn't like Dave, but one's
friends do tend to drift away when one is perceived to have a man. When Mother Grey let it slip
over the telephone that Dave was staying in Boston for another week, Deedee insisted on coming
to Fishersville for the weekend. "I'll be there in
two hours," she said.

"You don't have to come and comfort me, Deedee. I'm not really as broken up as all that."

"I'm not coming to comfort you," she said. "I
want a game of Scrabble. Arthur is having a guest
preacher this weekend, and he told me I could
take Sunday off." Arthur was Canon Arthur Spelving, rector of Holy Assumption in Ocean Prospect
and Deedee's boss.

And so while Mother Grey was marrying Celia
Warthen to Anthony Rossi, Deedee had arrived at
the rectory, let herself in with the key under the
false rock, and made herself comfortable. Mother
Grey came in and found her reading in front of
the fire, a perfect picture for a winter's evening.
She was ensconced in the flowered chair under
the cuckoo clock Mother Grey had brought back
from Bavaria, her feet on the flowered ottoman,
the afghan around her shoulders, her gray hair in
a knot on top of her head, her face like an apple
in the firelight. A mug of hot coffee was at her

elbow, Towser was snoring by her side. She looked like Mrs. Santa Claus.

"You look awfully comfortable," said Mother Grey. "But you know we have to go out in an hour to a shower for Saraleigh Kane." Towser jumped up and came to her, and she gave him his canapés.

Deedee sighed and put down the book, yet another paperback western by Louis L'Amour. She must have brought it with her. Mother Grey never read such stuff. "Too bad," Deedee said. "It's a great day to curl up with a good book."

"What do you see in those things?" Mother Grey asked her.

"He tells a great story. The elements are very satisfying."

"What elements?"

"The mountain pass, the coffee, the degenerate bad guy, the clean-living Indian warrior, the noble western maiden, the faithful horse."

"What mountain pass?"

"The cowboy is forced to take his horse on a shortcut over a mountain trail so narrow that one stirrup brushes the rocky wall of the cliff face and the other hangs out over a two-thousand-foot drop."

"Thrilling. He does this in every book?"

"Of course not. That would be boring. Just often enough so that you look for it."

"Tell me about the western maiden. A pale subservient creature, I suppose."

"Oh, no, no. Tanned. Weather-beaten, even. Able to load rifles in an Indian fight and ride and shoot when she has to. Fit to breed a race of warriors. You know the type. She always falls for the hero at first sight, but they never kiss, at least not until after the book is over."

"In every book?"

"Sometimes he rides away without her at the end. Call of the wild and all that. Sometimes she even dies. And then again, a number of the books don't have her in them at all."

"Do you miss her when that happens?"

"Not at all. The cowboy's real relationship is with the faithful horse anyway."

"Ah."

"Very important element. The faithful mustang, trained to stand still when the cowboy drops the reins to the ground, and to come when he whistles."

"Not like the horses I've encountered."

"No, real horses are a fractious and willful species. But not Louis L'Amour horses. They always mind. Also, they warn him of danger. Of course, the cowboy is very attentive to his horse, and it helps."

"What's your favorite thing about these books?"

"The coffee."

"Cowboy coffee."

"The cowboy can be lying out in the weeds somewhere, wounded in seven places from his latest battle with bad guys or Indians, and the first thing he does when he comes to is to scrape together a few twigs to start a fire for coffee."

"Powerful."

"Must be. You never see him smoke or drink alcohol, though. You hardly ever even see him eat. But he can't stay alive without his java. So what is this shower?"

"You know that Ralph and Saraleigh are to be married next week, right?"

"Yes."

"Martine Wellworth is giving Saraleigh a surprise wedding shower tonight."

"Martine. The black lawyer from Newark."

"Please. African American. And she isn't from Newark, she just works there. She's from Harlem."

"I thought she was West Indian."

"Her husband is West Indian. Albert. Their son is named Henry. I baptized him." You wouldn't have thought, with so few people in the parish, that Mother Grey would have to keep describing them over and over again to her best friend. But Deedee was forty-seven, after all. They say the approach of menopause makes you forgetful.

"Is Martine a friend of Saraleigh's?" Deedee said.

"They are friends. It does seem strange, now that I think of it. Saraleigh is so . . ."

"Coarse," Deedee prompted.

"Now, Deedee. I was going to say Saraleigh is so uneducated, such a princess of the underclass with her tattoos and her cigarettes and chewing gum. Martine is so dignified. I don't really think they have much in common, but they do have children the same age, and that always seems to make a bond between women."

"So Martine is giving her a shower."

"I told her I thought it was awfully good of her to go to all this trouble for Saraleigh, with her busy schedule. She said she was having fun. She seldom does frivolous things anymore, she said; the last time she gave somebody a shower, it was one of her roommates at Howard."

"What did you get for a shower gift?"

"Martine said she was giving her some sort of outrageous lingerie."

"Lewd underwear! Just the thing for a mother of three children by three different fathers," said Deedee.

"That's how I felt about it, but I kept my opinions to myself. For my part, I'm giving the bride a set of cookware."

"Will Martine mind if I come along?"

"Of course not."

"And Saraleigh will be surprised."

"Saraleigh is always surprised by any sort of kindness."

"Is there anything we have to do first?" Deedee asked.

"Wrap presents. Bake muffins."

"Muffins."

"It's no big deal. I always make muffins for potluck occasions because I can do them from a mix, and I have these tiny little pans. People like little bitty muffins, and they aren't any work.

Come out and talk to me while I do them." Deedee slipped into her shoes and made her way to the kitchen without waking the dog.

The kitchen was smaller than the one in the old rectory but still comfortable for sitting. Mother Grey stirred the batter while Deedee buttered the pans. There were a few small items of diocesan gossip to be chewed over while the oven heated; nothing major—politics in Trenton were as cool as everything else right then.

When she had put the muffins in the oven, Mother Grey sat down and described the wedding reception, how she had come upon her acolyte reading what appeared to be a little black book, how a dealer had offered her money for St. Bede's furnishings. "And then the father of the bride made a pass at me," she concluded. The timer went *ding!* and she removed the muffins. So much for cooking.

"Happens all the time," said Deedee.

"It does?"

"The guy is a Wasp, right?"

"Well, yes; it's the Episcopal Church, after all."

"Sure, but it doesn't always follow. He's an uptight Wasp."

"I prefer to think of him as a rich stiff."

"Okay. He's a rich stiff, and he is so far out of touch with his feelings that he isn't even aware that he has any. Now his eldest daughter gets married."

"Only."

"I beg your pardon?"

"His only daughter. They have one girl and one boy."

"Okay, whatever. So what does a man with no feelings that he is aware of do at his only daughter's wedding? First he follows the program as outlined by his wife and the caterer, but eventually he comes to the end of that script. It wasn't satisfying. By that time he's had too much to drink, so he finds himself acting out unexpectedly. Either he picks a fight, or he makes a pass at some inappropriate person, such as one of the bride's friends, or the priest's wife, or the priest."

"Have you been to a lot of weddings of rich stiffs, then?"

"One too many," said Deedee. Mother Grey understood her to mean her own. Shortly before Deedee decided to study for the priesthood, her husband of twenty years deserted her for a cupcake from his office. Mother Grey inferred from the little that Deedee said about him that he never was any great shakes as a husband, but as an ex he was even worse. After he was married to the cupcake, he would drink to excess and telephone Deedee in the middle of the night to whine about the way his life was turning out. A light sleeper, Mother Grey herself used to take those calls sometimes in the days when she and Deedee were rooming together. *That man is a ministry*, she would to say to herself, after talking him into getting off the phone, by which she meant he was a burden to everyone.

As for Deedee, she showed no signs of scarring

from the whole mess except for a slight cynicism on the subject of Holy Matrimony. It was true that she was somewhat overweight and perhaps too young at forty-seven to have gone completely gray, but this might have happened in spite of the feckless Caldwell Gilchrist and not because of him.

Mother Grey's preparations for the shower were almost complete. She went to find wrapping paper for her shower gift, and as she rummaged through the stationery drawer, she found herself thinking of the little black book.

"Do you know anything about old books?" she asked Deedee.

"How old?"

"Very."

"Not a whole lot. Old books aren't my line."

"What can you tell me about a little black book called Grim something-or-other?"

"Could that be *Grimorium Verum*?"

"I suppose it might be."

"That would be one of the grimoires, the classic sorcerer's spell books. Once upon a time you could be burned at the stake for reading such things. You don't think your little acolyte is getting into Satanism, do you, Vinnie?"

"I'm not aware of any Satanist cults in Fishersville," she said.

"Don't worry. If they're around, you'll see traces, and they won't be subtle. Last month the Satanists in Ocean Prospect got into Holy Assumption and left an incredible mess."

"Satanists broke into your church?"

"One of the things they do in some communities is to break into churches and hold perverse services. It seems to involve dripping candle wax in patterns all over the carpeting and sacrificing animals. They dragged out our black vestments and got chicken blood on them. It was just disgusting. But you know what?"

"What?"

"I don't have a present for Saraleigh."

"The secondhand bookstore is still open," said Mother Grey. "Maybe you could find her a good cookbook."

"Good idea." Deedee was always up for a visit to a source of cheap Louis L'Amour novels.

They suited up in their heavy clothes. Towser wanted to come, too, but the storm was howling and Mother Grey knew the dog would not be happy outside, even for the four-block walk from here to the Fishersville Bookseller. As she was locking the front door to the rectory, the telephone rang. *Let the answering machine get it,* she said to herself, and marched forth into the driving sleet.

The warm and slightly moldy interior of the Fishersville Bookseller was a welcome refuge. Peter Susswald, the bookseller himself, sat behind the cash register; he was engrossed in conversation with a bearded man in seedy tweeds.

While Deedee disappeared into the stacks to browse through the cookbooks—or perhaps to look for westerns—Mother Grey flipped through

the boxes of old vinyl recordings and tried to ig-
nore the men's murmured conversation. When
she noticed that Peter's customer was whining
about the deterioration of his musical skills, it
captured her attention. "My music is suffering,"
he was saying, "because I don't get a chance to
play that often anymore."

Mother Grey was unable to restrain herself.
She said to him, "You shouldn't even be here. You
should be home practicing."

He stared at her, trying to figure whether he
knew her and why she was speaking to him.

"Do you know how many people there are in
the world today? Have you any idea how many of
them are gifted musicians, or how few places
there are in the world of professional music for
those musicians? You need to practice every day.
Talking about it won't improve your skills."

"Guess I'll go home then," he said. Slowly he
backed toward the door. "See ya, Peter." Out he
went.

Peter Susswald stood up, unfolding himself
like a large Swiss army knife. He was very tall. He
grinned at her the way you would grin at a small
child who had just said something precocious.
"What made you say that to him, Mother Vinnie?
Just as a matter of curiosity."

"The Holy Spirit," she replied. It might have
been true.

"You haven't found a new cello yet, have you?"

"I would practice every day if only I had my
instrument again," she said. With God's grace she

might save enough to buy another one sometime. Right now other things came first; still, the lack of music in her life was ruining her disposition, causing her to attack perfect strangers in bookstores. "It just makes me tired," she said, "to run into these phony-baloney musicians who talk about it all the time but won't play unless somebody pays them. I hope he wasn't a very good friend of yours."

"Pretty good," Susswald said. "You called it, though—he's a phony-baloney musician. What can I do for you today?"

"Deedee is looking for a cookbook. I don't need anything except for some information, if you happen to have it."

Susswald was very knowledgeable about books; they said he had taught college English at one time before he became a merchant. "With pleasure," he said. "Information about what?"

"What do you know about a thing called *Grimorium Verum*?"

He was still for a long time, retrieving information from somewhere deep in his mind. "*Grimorium Verum*," he said at last. "The True Grimoire, allegedly published in Memphis by Alibeck the Egyptian, in the early sixteenth century. In fact, it was probably produced in Rome. It was supposed to contain the Clavicles of Solomon, as well as a number of spells and rosters of useful demons. It's a classic of its kind."

"How likely would I be to encounter such a thing here in town?"

"Extremely unlikely, I should say. It's a very rare book. I wasn't aware that there were any copies in this country, other than the one that was owned by J. P. Morgan."

"Why did he have it? Or are you going to try to tell me that J. P. Morgan used an ancient book of spells to make his fortune in banking?"

"No, no. Morgan was a collector of rare old books—one of the great collectors, in fact. No collection is really complete without the *Grimorium Verum*. I doubt whether he even tried to read it. It would be tough going even for a scholar. It's written in bad Latin and Old French mixed with gibberish."

Deedee called out from the back of the store: "Where do you keep the westerns?"

"Third shelf from the end," Susswald answered.

"Did you ever see it?" Mother Grey said.

"I went to see Morgan's books when they were on display several years ago. I didn't pay a whole lot of attention to the *Grimorium Verum*. There were other books that interested me more."

"Do you remember what it looked like?"

"Like your average little black book."

"I might have seen it myself today. I'm trying to decide whether it was real."

"In Fishersville?"

She laughed. "It would be strange, wouldn't it, to discover an authentic antique of any distinction in Fishersville?" The book dealer opened his mouth and raised his eyebrows, as though to defend his fellow dealers. "I'm sorry," she said hastily, "I didn't mean to cast aspersions on the local antique scene. What I meant was that some of the things they sell here for antiques are very attractive, and some may even be worth the price they're asking, but to find a rare old object with an authentic provenance here is probably unusual."

"Say not so!" he protested. "Fishersville is the antique capital of the Northeast!"

Deedee saved her from putting her foot any further into her mouth by emerging from the stacks with a cookbook and a handful of Louis L'Amours. "I'll get her this," she said, waving the cookbook. "There isn't a single reference in it to balsamic vinegar or extra-virgin olive oil."

"How is it on meat and potatoes?" said Mother Grey.

"Extremely robust." Deedee paid for the books. As they left, the bookseller locked up behind them. It was dark out already. The streetlights cast cone-shaped beams onto the snowy street that showed a fine precipitation.

A lone sprig of freesia dangling from the musicians' balcony was all that remained of the wedding reception decorations that had lately embellished the Umbrella Works. The caterers had removed the little tables and swept up the last lipstick-stained cocktail napkin. Lingering there to wind up a bit of business before locking up,

Simon Ratcher surveyed his domain with pleasure.

Sleet rattled against the expensive new windows. Noting how the wind found ways around the little panes of glass and through the mullions, he asked himself: *Should I have done the number with the big double-glazed windows, the way the first architect recommended?* No. Like the subdued lighting, little panes with mullions gave the place atmosphere. Without atmosphere it had nothing.

He turned his attention to the bronze bust of a young woman that the boy was presenting for his inspection. It was a piece of Victoriana with enormous charm, sporting a feathered hat and lace at the bodice. The lips were smiling coquettishly, little teeth glinting in the light of Ratcher's desk lamp. He put his hand on it. It was just as he remembered.

"Good," he said. "This is fine. Fifty dollars, I believe we said." He offered the boy two crisp twenties and a ten.

"You sure this is all it's worth?" the boy said as he took the money.

"Of course not. It's worth much more. But you can't get any more for it."

"You won't give me any more, you mean. It isn't as easy as you seem to think breaking into a library. It's worth more than fifty, I'm sure."

"We agreed on fifty. I have a buyer for the bust. You don't. Be reasonable, Adam." He took the boy's hand and closed his fingers over the money.

"Maybe I don't feel like it."

A tough guy. Ratcher chuckled. "What are you going to do, then, take it back to the library?"

The boy stared at him for a long moment, his brown eyes glowering under the dark fall of hair. Ratcher thought, *He wants to hit me.* The idea was exciting.

Suddenly the door creaked open, letting in the cold and the sound of softly hissing sleet. A stranger stood in the doorway in dripping clothes, gaping at the interior of Simon's store. He did not appear to be a man who enjoyed or could pay for rare objects. "May I help you?" Simon said, knowing the answer would be *No, I must have the wrong place.*

"I used to work here," the man said. "You changed it."

Simon laughed lightly. "That must have been when it was a real umbrella factory," he said. "Come in and look around if you want to."

He came in as the boy turned to go.

"I'll see you later, Adam," said Ratcher.

"No, you won't," said the boy. "That was it. This is the last time." He paused at the door, glanced at the stranger, and looked away as though he were a particularly boring piece of furniture. "That goes for the rest of us too," he said. "That goes for me and my friends. You can find somebody else to party with, you cheap asshole." He went out the door, slamming it, rattling the little windowpanes. Time would tell about his little friends, of course. Adam might find that they

47

were more loyal to Ratcher's good dope than they were to him.

The stranger was looking after the boy with one eyebrow up. Ratcher realized he thought he was witnessing something like a lover's quarrel.

"Guess you'll have to get it someplace else," the stranger said, his voice heavy with insolence.

Ratcher blinked, and then smirked at him. "How long have you been out?"

"Out?"

"I'm sorry. Something about you suggested to me that you had been in prison. Maybe it was the crude tattoo on your hand. My mistake."

"Where I been is my business."

"And where I get it, as you put it, is mine," said Ratcher. Then he had an idea. A recent ex-convict! "I might have some business for you, however, if you need work."

"Not in my line," said the stranger.

"I need something stolen."

"Steal it yourself."

"I'll pay you twenty-five hundred dollars. It's a very simple job, the work of an evening."

"What is it?"

"A brass processional crucifix. You can pick up anything else of value that you see around, just so no one thinks that's all you were after."

"Where do I find it?"

"In a church."

"I'll think about it and let you know. I have to go see somebody."

"I'll be here until six," Ratcher called after the

ex-con, who was already plunging out the door and into the weather. *He may yet do this job for me,* thought Ratcher. At least he hadn't flinched from the idea of burglarizing a church. If he wanted to turn him in to the law, which seemed unlikely, it would merely be Ratcher's word against his.

The message waiting on her answering machine when Mother Grey returned to the rectory was from Dave Dogg. His voice was strange and tentative, even distant. He said he just wanted to talk, and left a number; the area code was for Boston. Music played in the background, something completely vapid and irritating, New Age probably. Had Dave Dogg taken to listening to New Age music? What was happening to him up there?

There was no answer when she dialed the number; she let it ring twelve times.

While Deedee was wrapping the cookbook for Saraleigh, Mother Grey went over in her mind the things Peter Susswald, the bookseller, had told her about the little black book. She realized suddenly that she had no idea what the Clavicles of Solomon might be. Should she wait for the store to reopen on Monday and go back and ask him? No. She should look it up in *Webster's Third New International Dictionary*, as Granny had taught her to do.

The dictionary was no help. The only definition for *clavicle* that was offered there was of the bone. Surely Alibeck the Egyptian hadn't pretended to grind up King Solomon's clavicles to make paper. Or had he? Of course it would give the thing an air of great magical power. Splinters of the True Cross. The Clavicles of Solomon.

What else could it be? *Clavicle* meant key. She looked up *key of Solomon* and found nothing, although there was a reference to *key of art*—see *alembroth*. Ah! This was more like it. *Alembroth* was a name used by the alchemists for double chloride of ammonium and mercury. They believed it to be a universal solvent and also called it *salt of wisdom*. She looked up *salt of this and that* and found a number of other names used by alchemists to identify various chemicals and allude to their mystical properties. Was this to the point? Or not?

Perhaps the *Clavicle of Solomon* was a list of poisons.

"All wrapped," said Deedee, flourishing her recipe book. "Let's go."

They took Deedee's car to go and fetch Delight van Buskirk, whose job it was to sit with the babies while the party took place, because Deedee's car had four-wheel drive. It was not as bad as they were expecting. Rock Hill Road had been plowed, salted, and sanded only minutes before.

"This is a piece of cake," said Deedee. "I thought you said the driving would be bad."

"Delight van Buskirk lives right in the middle of Fisher's Pointe," said Mother Grey. "The condo dwellers need a lot of maintenance from the city

50

of Fishersville. They're helpless without their municipal services."

"She lives in a yuppie condo?"

"She lives in an old farmhouse," said Mother Grey. "They built the condos around her."

Mrs. van Buskirk was waiting by the door. When the old lady came out, they saw that she had metal prongs strapped to her boots to keep from falling down on the ice.

"Those are nice," said Deedee. "I wish I had a pair. Where did you get them, Mrs. van Buskirk?"

"They belonged to my father," she said. "This is the first year I've needed them in a long time." They discussed the weather on the way down into town. Mrs. van Buskirk herself had never seen a winter like this, she said, and she was ninety-four. "I hope it clears up for Saraleigh's wedding."

"I'm sure Saraleigh's wedding will be wonderful no matter what the weather," said Mother Grey.

"Too bad about the church organ," said Mrs. van Buskirk. "It would be so nice to have some music. Do you suppose it will ever work again?"

"I'll have to take a look at it," said Mother Grey. "Maybe we can get it working with less trouble than we think. The problem is finding someone to play it. It's not as easy as a piano."

"You could hire someone," suggested Deedee.

"No way to pay 'em."

"Maybe you could get the Warthens to kick in."

"That would be lovely," said Mrs. van Buskirk.

The Warthens, of course, were not fond of Saraleigh and Ralph and tolerated them only because a Christian was supposed to. Finance their wedding?

"Lovely," agreed Mother Grey. "But it seems so unlikely."

It wasn't that long ago that Mrs. van Buskirk herself had had no use for Saraleigh. The tattoos, the chewing gum, the clothes, the language, all were extremely off-putting. Under Saraleigh's horrifying exterior, however, beat a warm and generous heart. It was she who had saved the church when Mother Grey was in the hospital, rounding up everyone in town to come to services the morning the Archdeacon came to close it down. After that, Mrs. van Buskirk became very friendly toward her. As for Saraleigh's children, illegitimate they might be, but the old lady was crazy about them, the new baby most of all. Her own grandchildren were nearly grown up.

It took a while to get Mrs. van Buskirk up the two flights of stairs to Saraleigh's apartment. "I can still do it," she said, "but I have to take it slowly." At last they reached the top and knocked at the door.

The wedding shower, in classic style, involved an elaborate deception to get the bride to the party, so that when Saraleigh opened the door, releasing a gust of apartment-reek—cabbage, cigarette butts, diapers—she was dressed to go to the Acme, in skintight stretch pants and a pink midriff sweater, with her yellow hair hanging straight instead of frizzed and only one tattoo showing. Had she but known they were on their way to a party in her honor, Saraleigh would have been wearing her best dress, cut up to here and down to there. It was just as well. Mother Grey actually preferred Saraleigh's "casual" look to the startling getups she wore for formal occasions.

It suddenly occurred to Mother Grey that, for the first time since she had known her, Saraleigh looked completely happy.

"Hi. Come in," she said. "I'll get my coat. The baby's asleep, Mrs. van Buskirk, but you can play with Britney." She stubbed out her cigarette and slipped on her coat.

The old lady took the little girl on her knee, tickled her under the chin, and began to recite Mother Goose verses. " 'Wee Willie Winkie runs through the town, upstairs and downstairs, in his nightgown.' " Britney giggled and clapped. The old rhyme sounded almost like an incantation to Mother Grey, and she thought about Edward and his spells.

"There's cake in the refrigerator," Saraleigh said. "If you get hungry. But we won't be very long."

" 'Rapping at the window, crying through the lock, are the children in their beds? For it's now eight o'clock.' Have a good time."

"Thanks," said Saraleigh, "but it's only the Acme."

She closed the door. On their way down the stairs, they could still hear the old lady's voice:

" 'Here comes a candle to light you to bed,
" 'Here comes a chopper to chop off your head.' "

Officer Jack Kreevitch looked up from his desk in the basement of City Hall to see Rex Perskie coming down the concrete steps, taking them two at a time. It was almost like seeing a ghost. The effect was intensified when Perskie opened the door, letting in a blast of wind as cold as death that rattled the venetian blinds and ruffled Kreevitch's hair.

"Brother Rex," Kreevitch said.

"Yo, Jack."

"You're looking good, Rex." Perskie was standing up a lot taller than he had been the last time Kreevitch saw him, the time Kreevitch had had to take his gun away and run him in for threatening Saraleigh. They must have kept him off the sauce in prison. His shoulders were bigger, he looked healthier. He looked good. But Kreevitch could not honestly say it was good to see him.

He seemed to be all wet. "Take off your coat. Hang it over the radiator. How are you doing?"

"Not bad." Perskie took off his outer garments. "I'm looking for a job. You guys need anybody to check parking meters or like that?"

Chief Harry hire a jailbird? Not likely. "You'll have to ask Chief Harry."

"Is he in?"

54

Kreevitch pressed a button on the new intercom the city had bought them when they got the block grant. "Hey, Chief. You in? I got Rex Perskie out here. He wants to talk to you."

Chief Harry said, "Send him in." By leaving the intercom on, Kreevitch was able to overhear their conversation, brief as it was.

"Chief Harry. You need any help?" Perskie said.

"You looking to get back in uniform, Rex?"

"Yeah, if you—"

"Still drinking?"

"No, I—"

"Didn't you just spend eighteen months in prison?"

"Uh—"

"I don't think I need anybody right now, buddy."

"Well, keep me in mind if you get an opening," said Perskie, backing out of the office.

"Right," said the chief. Kreevitch turned the intercom off as Perskie closed Chief Harry's door.

Shame about Rex. He hadn't been a bad cop, not really. When he was sober. At other times he was a problem, which was how come they'd kicked him off the force. Kreevitch remembered going up Reeker's Hill in the snow looking for Rex to bust him for arson. He felt almost guilty now for suspecting Rex of setting those fires. As it turned out, it was two other guys. Maybe if people in town weren't always thinking Rex was bad, he wouldn't have gone down to that bar in Florida

Kate Gallison

and beat up the politician's son or whoever he was, and had to do time.

The steam had stopped rising from the coat. Perskie felt it and, seeming satisfied with its condition, slipped it on. "So where can I find Saraleigh these days?" he said, as if casually.

"What do you want with Saraleigh?"

Perskie said, "She's my woman, Jack. That baby is mine, I'm pretty sure."

"Not hardly, bro. Kid was born last month. You been away awhile."

"I meant Britney. What, has she got another one?"

"Another girl. They named her after the preacher."

"What preacher?"

"Mother Grey."

"Saraleigh named her baby Mother Grey?"

"No, Lavinia. Vinnie. She's doing all right, Rex. You should just let her be. Mother Grey taught her to type and stuff. She's going to get a job any day now."

"Your ass."

"She and this guy she's living with are gonna get married. Let her alone. She has her life now, you take care of yours. Friendly advice, Rex."

"Right. Oh, by the way, you still got my old service revolver?"

"Yeah. It's in the evidence closet. Why?"

"Could you let me have it back?"

"I dunno, Rex. What do you want it for?"

"Come on, gimme it. It ain't evidence of

nothin'. I didn't do nothin'. I just want to get my stuff and move on."

"You're not staying in Fishersville?"

"Shit, no. Where would I stay? If, like you say, Saraleigh won't have me back. I'm goin' back where it's warm, man. Where the weather suits my clothes. Gimme my piece."

Kreevitch gave him the gun. Safe enough, he thought; it wasn't loaded. Bullets for a .357 Magnum were practically impossible to find in Fishersville these days, especially for a convicted felon. By the time Rex Perskie loaded that bad boy again, he would be a long, long way from here.

From the police station Perskie went to Rooney's, the old bar where he used to drink. He found it dripping with ferns. Arnie wasn't tending bar there anymore, and Perskie didn't know the new guy. He didn't know anybody in there. It was full of yuppies. He had a beer and moved on down the street, when suddenly he came across the new bar, the real bar where everybody had gone after the old bar filled up with greenery.

There were all his old drinking companions to welcome him. There was Arnie behind the bar. "Gimme the usual," he said. Home at last.

"So, Arnie," he said as he paid for the whiskey, "what do you hear from Saraleigh? Where's she living these days?"

"Over on Elm Street," the bartender said.

"That apartment house where Jimmy Finn used to live. You know the one? The Fairview."

"Yeah, I know it. Thanks." The bartender leaned closer to Perskie and lowered his eyes and his voice. "You knew she was getting married, right?"

"Was," Perskie said. "Was getting married." The gun felt almost good, tucked into its old place in his back waistband. "By the way, you seen Murph lately?"

"Not for months," said the bartender. "Why?"

"Sometimes I used to buy bullets from him. Thought I'd do some target shooting. Know anybody else who might have some?"

"No, man," said Arnie. "Can't help you there." His manner had cooled suddenly. Perskie ordered another whiskey to allay any suspicions the bartender might have.

Never mind, he could take care of business with his bare hands. He finished the drink and put a tip on the bar for Arnie. Time to clean house on Saraleigh and her new boyfriend.

"Surprise!"

The scene that met the eyes of Mother Grey, Saraleigh, and Deedee Gilchrist when they opened Martine Wellworth's door was one of merry conviviality. Balloons and streamers hung from the walls and ceiling of Martine's jewellike living room where thirty or forty friends and neighbors, most of them women, were crammed in together. Mother Grey knew most of them, some from the church, others from around town. Judging from their lusty shouts and the punch cups they were waving, they had been partying for some time before the arrival of the guest of honor.

Martine, slender and lovely in a one-piece hostess thing with floppy pants, rushed up and hugged Saraleigh and then took her by the arm and sat her on the sofa under the lacy umbrella next to her betrothed. Saraleigh was plump, but Ralph was—let's face it—fat, and looked even bigger and fatter in this roomful of women. He put down whatever it was he was eating long enough to give Saraleigh a kiss. She looked at all the presents and started to cry.

Somebody gave her a tissue. Somebody else handed her a big plate full of food. Mother Grey took her muffins to the kitchen, where she hovered in the doorway at the edge of the hubbub while Saraleigh unwrapped with squeals of delight four woks, a black lace peignoir, a set of conventional cookware, a cookbook, and a fifty-dollar gift certificate from the Kmart. Completely happy.

Marla Kreevitch, Martine's neighbor from across the street, was hovering in the kitchen along with Mother Grey. Liberated for the moment from her five children, she seemed to enjoy standing somewhere quiet. "I just realized how well Saraleigh looks," Mother Grey said to her. "Happy and at peace with herself. Did Jack ever tell you about the night she came to my house with the children because Rex said he was going to shoot her?"

"They did that all the time, Mother Vinnie," said Marla. "Jack was always having to go over to their place and break up some big fight. Then she would never file charges."

"It's a good thing he's gone," said Mother Grey. Jack Kreevitch's wife looked uncomfortable. "Is something wrong?"

"No, no."

"What is it?"

"Nothing. Just that Jack came home tonight and said, 'Guess who I saw today? Rex Perskie.' "

When she spoke, the party noises came to a momentary silence, and Rex's name hung in the air like a sudden bad smell.

Marla Kreevitch cleared her throat, then lowered her voice and the party went on. "He was looking for work, but Chief Harry wouldn't hire him. Jack had a long talk with him, told him to forget about Saraleigh and get out of Fishersville. So I'm sure he's gone by now."

4

The apartments in the Fairview had front doors and back doors, as Rex remembered from the old days when Jimmy Finn used to live there. He checked the names at the front and then went up two flights of back stairs and tried the handle of Saraleigh's kitchen door. It was locked. He rapped on the glass.

After some delay the porch light went on, and an incredibly old lady appeared at the door with an afghan around her shoulders. She put the chain on and cracked the door a little. "Yes?" she said.

"I want Saraleigh," he said.

"She isn't home. Can I give her a message?"

"When is she coming home?"

"I couldn't say."

This wasn't the way he'd planned it. In his plan he kicked in the door, beat the crap out of the new man, and moved in. He could still kick down the door, of course. He could even beat the crap out of this old lady, but it wouldn't be the same. The act of bursting in and forcing his will on the household would be so much more satisfying if Saraleigh were there.

"Tell her I'll be back," he said.

"And who might you be?"

"Her husband."

"No you're not. Ah! I remember you now. You're that nasty little Rex Perskie. We all hoped you'd left town forever. Saraleigh doesn't live here anymore." She slammed the door and drew the bolt.

"Fuck you, lady," he said. He went back down the stairs. So she was out catting around tonight. If it wasn't so friggin' cold, he would wait behind one of these bushes and jump out at her when she came home. But she could be out all night. He might freeze to death. He would get her tomorrow. Or later, after he got hold of some bullets for this gun.

It was time to find someplace to spend the night. He could always hike up Reeker's Hill and sleep in one of the wrecked cars, but it would be better to have heat.

Suddenly he thought of the factory, all fixed up now, heated and full of soft furniture. He could break in and sleep in one of that old pervert's secondhand beds.

DEVIL'S WORKSHOP

It took a while to find the best way in. The main entrance was strong and well-locked. There might even have been a burglar alarm. Perskie went all around the building, stumbling over the woodpile, using matches for light, getting snow in his shoes, before discovering that the last cellar window on the side by the river was loose. He borrowed an ax from the woodpile and used it to pry the window sash entirely out of its frame.

A life of crime, he thought. *This is the first step.* Beating up that guy in Florida didn't count. Now it was breaking and entering; next would come the hit on the church . . . but all this was dumb stuff. What he really needed was a big score, big enough to finance a good life with his woman, somewhere far from Fishersville.

He put the ax back, nearly cutting himself on it, it was so sharp. Then he crawled in through the window and put the sash back in the frame more or less the way it had been. The cellar had a dirt floor. There was a sharp smell of mildew and rats, and a sound of dripping. He struck another match and began to look for the stairs.

Doors lined one wall of the narrow space. Perskie opened them one by one, revealing Simon Ratcher to be a man of many hobbies.

The first door led to a room a little bigger than a closet, with a stainless-steel sink. Perskie flipped the wall switch; bloodred light showed it to be a photographic darkroom: chemicals, trays, an enlarger. Hanging from a line, five-by-eight black and white photos of young boys doing it in a chapel. Revolted, he switched off the light again. Then something made him take one of the hanging pictures. The kid with the dark hair could have been the one who was there earlier. He folded it and put it in his pocket.

The next door led to the chapel.

When Perskie switched the light on, he thought, *This guy is a piece of work.* His secret little church had an altar, all right, but what hung over it wasn't any statue of Jesus. And yet some of the stuff in there looked real, like what you would find in a real church. So that's why he wanted stuff stolen from churches.

Since his matches were running low, he took a candelabra and lit the candles, then turned out the light to see the effect. The light of the candles was absorbed at once by black velvet draperies. Here and there the image of a Satanic goat face or inverted pentagram glimmered in the darkness. Creepy. He closed the door and moved on.

The third door was a broom closet, full of ordinary brooms and cleaning supplies. The fourth door opened onto the stairs. He went up them and found himself in the business office of the store. This was more like it, warm and dry. He could even sleep right here on the couch.

The desk was locked. There was a small safe under the desk, and it was locked too. All these locks. The guy must have plenty to protect. He took one of the business cards from the Lucite holder on the desk and read it: *The Umbrella Works, Fishersville, New Jersey, Simon Ratcher,*

Antiques and Collectibles. He put it back in the holder.

There were cigars in a humidor; Perskie took one and lit it on a candle. Too bad Ratcher didn't keep any whiskey in his office. Perskie sat down on the old-time swivel chair and put his feet up on the desk. He slipped the picture of the two boys out of his coat pocket, unfolded it, and looked at it, then put it back in again. An idea came to him. Maybe it would be possible to make some money off Ratcher, above and beyond what the guy was willing to give him to steal things.

He could be blackmailed.

Perskie got up and took the candelabra out into the main area of the store. It was cold and drafty, the air currents making the candles flicker and casting moving shadows of the furniture and the staircases. The wind howled outside, and the old factory creaked. Although the river was right there, not twenty yards away, Perskie could hear no sound of water. It must be about frozen over. From within the factory came sounds, creaking, gnawing, little scuttling noises.

It was warmer back in the office, warmer still with the door closed. He put the cigar on the edge of the desk and stretched out on the couch. As he framed an elaborate plan to rip off Simon Ratcher, he drifted off to sleep. The noises were nowhere near as unrestful as the night sounds in Florida State Prison.

*   *   *

When Simon Ratcher came into his office to catch up on some bookkeeping before the store opened, he found his tame ex-convict asleep on his couch. The man reeked; he hadn't bathed in days. There were cigar ashes on the rug, sweat stains on the silk sofa pillows. Wax from the candelabra (what was that doing up here?) had run down and congealed on the varnished desktop. Ratcher shook him roughly by the shoulder. He blinked awake, saw who was shaking him, and sat up slowly, stretching his arms.

"Can you think of any reason why I shouldn't call the police and have you arrested for breaking and entering?" Ratcher said.

"Go for it, Pops. Or should I call you Father?"

"What do you mean?"

"With that little setup you got downstairs, I thought you might be running a church."

"You've got more nerve than I would have guessed," said Ratcher.

"I liked the pictures of your altar boys."

"Are you going to do that job for me that I asked you about?"

"Sure, why not. But maybe we should be talking about a little more money. I got a woman to support now." He drew something out of his pocket, a photograph, rumpled but recognizable. It was not a picture of a woman, but one of Simon's own pictures.

So that was the way the wind blew. *It seems that I'll have to take steps*, thought Ratcher. "Perhaps we can arrange something," he said. "How much do you want?"

The ex-con blinked. After a pause he said, "How about ten thousand dollars?"

"For what?"

"You know what."

"No. Tell me. I want to hear it. For doing a job for me? For keeping quiet? For dropping dead? What?"

"I ain't gonna drop dead for you. Sorry."

"A pity. All right then, ten thousand dollars for burglarizing the church, giving me what I want from it, and leaving town." He made a grab for the picture of the boys, but the ex-con dodged him and put it back in his pocket. "And giving me that picture."

"Okay," the man said. "Sounds good."

Ratcher gave him directions to St. Bede's. It seemed to him that a flicker of interest crossed the man's face when he heard what church he was expected to rob, but it might have been a trick of the light. He described the processional crucifix. "Take whatever else you see that might be valuable," Ratcher added. "Make it look like a random burglary. I'm sure you can manage that."

"Sure, why not."

"I'll have the money for you when you come back. Incidentally, I don't want to see you again before you do this job."

"No, huh? How about an advance?"

"Sorry. I don't keep a lot of money around. You have to leave now; I'll be getting customers in here soon. Use the back door through the sculpture garden. That way no one will see you go. I'm sure you know where the back door is. You seem to have made yourself entirely at home here."

The ex-con's only reply to all this was an unpleasant snicker. He made his way out while Ratcher watched him. *Now he'll go rob the church*, thought Ratcher, *and then he'll come back here*.

And then Ratcher would carry out the rest of his plan. The shotgun under the cash register counter was entirely legal. He actually had a permit to own it. No one would fault him for killing a burglar in self-defense, and if some of the burglar's loot got lost—say, a processional crucifix—and if a picture happened to disappear from the burglar's pocket, who would be the wiser?

But since it was Sunday morning, it would probably be a while before the ex-con was able to carry out his mission; right at this moment the targeted church was probably full of worshipers. Ratcher didn't really expect the ex-con to return before nightfall, when the deserted church would be an easy mark. Then Ratcher would be here waiting for him. He turned his attention to the bookkeeping but found that he was too uneasy in his mind to concentrate. It always calmed him to look after his treasures, so he picked up a feather duster and began to dust.

Mother Grey and Ralph were also spiffing up, sweeping away little bits of flower petals and rice after the wedding. As they prepared for Sunday services, Mother Grey noticed the processional crucifix, coveted object of local dealers, showing signs of tarnish. She set Ralph Voercker to polishing it.

"The altar rail could use a touch too," she said, "as long as you have the brass polish out."

"Maybe there's not enough time," said Ralph. "People will be getting here soon."

"Right," said Mother Grey. "There's not enough time." The church still wore the festive air of a wedding; the more extravagant floral decorations had been removed, but several arrangements remained piled up around the altar, and the freesia perfumed the sanctuary.

"Do you think these flowers will still be okay for our wedding next Saturday?" Ralph asked.

"We can but hope," said Mother Grey, slipping into her vestments. "Water them when you get a chance."

She was expecting Deedee to come over any minute to help her serve Communion. *I hope she's up*, Mother Grey thought. She had last seen her friend fast asleep in the guest bed with her long gray braid outside the covers. Deedee was always late for things. Maybe she would sleep in and not show up at all. As Mother Grey was having these thoughts, Deedee herself came rushing in, disheveled and breathless as usual.

"There's a truck pulled up on the rectory lawn," she said. "You'd better come see about this."

"What in the world?"

"Two youths have backed a pickup truck right up to the rectory. I think they're up to no good."

Mother Grey put her head out the side door to see the four-wheel-drive pickup from Bountiful Horse Farms parked in what she liked to think of as her garden. "Rodman Sedgewick strikes again," she muttered.

"Who?" said Deedee.

"Lord Bountiful."

Sedgewick's sons, Chip and Lance, were wrestling a large white object out of the back of their truck. She waded out into the snow and confronted them. "What's this?"

"Dad said you might need this freezer, Mother Grey," said Lance, without pausing in his efforts. "Easy, Chip. Just a little more to the right—"

"A freezer?" *But I don't even cook.*

"He said if you didn't need it for the day-care center, you could maybe sell it. (Ah! That does it. Good, Chip.) You can keep the money for the church. They'll just take the tax write-off."

The freezer was not the upright kind but lay on its long end like a six-passenger enameled mausoleum. It filled the entire side yard. "I don't know what to say."

"It's only ten years old," said Chip. "It works too. Where shall we put it?"

"How about back in the truck?" said Mother Grey.

The boys chuckled. "We'll just leave it here till you figure out where you want it," said Lance.

"Holds twenty-two cubic feet," said Chip. "The scratches are just superficial."

"He said to try to keep it full," said Lance. "It runs more economically. Here's the key." He handed her a small cylindrical key on a key chain, and she stood holding it in the palm of her hand. Words failed her. "He said don't thank him. He was glad to do it."

Thank him? "Tell him not to worry," said Mother Grey as the boys jumped back in the truck and scratched out of her dormant flower bed. She wrung her hands, muttered, "My word," and went back to the church, only to encounter the Warthens on their way in the side door.

You would never know from Major Warthen's bland smile and hearty handshake that he had tried to put a hickey on Mother Grey's neck the day before. Probably he had forgotten. He did seem a little hung over; his eyes were bloodshot, and there was a stale odor of alcohol still on his breath.

Perhaps he had blackouts. Did the major have an alcohol problem? Mother Grey watched the family walk down the aisle together and thought, *Hmm*. She had never considered the Warthens a troubled family, but you never knew. Young Edward, her new acolyte, liked to spend so much time in the church that she'd given him a key so he could come in and polish the brass. Was the boy fleeing an unpleasant home situation? Mother Grey was fond of the child because he was so beautiful, with his blue eyes and halo of golden curls. But truth to tell, she had no notion of what went on in his head.

Maybe the major was a problem to his family. Maybe he regularly got tight in public and tried to kiss women on the neck. Or maybe Deedee was right, and the major merely an ordinary middle-class Wasp reacting in typical fashion to the marriage of his only daughter.

They could talk about it later, before Deedee left to go back to Ocean Prospect. It was good to have Deedee around for discussions like this. Dave Dogg was no good for gossipy chats about the parishioners; as a cop, a man, and a working-class person, his outlook was all wrong. Mother Grey could just hear him: *What do you mean, the stiff tried to give you a hickey?* Actually she wasn't sure whether he would get mad or laugh. Maybe she would call that number again when church was over. It would be good to hear his voice.

At least, she hoped it would be good. Perhaps he had something unpleasant to say to her.

Fifteen parishioners and a visiting stranger were there to join in the opening hymn. Mother Grey led them as best she could a cappella, since there was no one to play the organ, even if it had been in working order. It was a good crowd for a bad-weather Sunday. Saraleigh and the babies weren't in church, but she understood from Ralph that Britney had a cold and Saraleigh didn't want to take her out. Maybe she would check in on them later.

DEVIL'S WORKSHOP

* * *

As Freddy Kane lay on the sofa playing with G.I. Joes, thinking maybe he would go out in a little while and play in the snow, he thought he heard the back door open. The Joes made a rush up over his kneecap, charging the Cobra enemy. "Yo, Joe!" Freddy muttered, speaking the battle cry softly to keep the game private from his mother in the kitchen. "Attack! Attack! Eat lead, Cobra scum." The Cobra forces retreated down his shin.

Then he felt a cold current of air, and suddenly Freddy had a bad feeling. Worse than a feeling, it was a smell, familiar and unmistakable, partly whiskey and partly men's armpits, reminding him of beatings and other ugly things from when he was little. Rex was back. They must have let him out of jail. The smell seemed to be coming from the back of the apartment.

Slowly, silently, Freddy sat up, spilling soldiers into the cracks between the cushions. Carefully he moved to where he could see into the kitchen. Rex was standing at the screen door looking in at Freddy's mom.

"Hi, babe," Rex said. "I'm home."

Freddy remembered Rex as being thinner. Now he was all covered with hard-looking muscles. Freddy's mom said to him, "You got a new tattoo. Do it yourself?"

"Friend of mine in the joint," Rex said.

"The joint. Nice," said Mom.

"You gonna let me in?"

Don't let him in, Freddy pleaded silently. *Please, please, please don't let him in.* Almost as if she heard him, his mom said, "No, Rex. I ain't gonna let you in. You don't live here." She shut the door and put the chain on it.

Freddy should have known that a simple refusal wouldn't work on Rex. Even when he hadn't had muscles, he could have just kicked that door in, and now all it took was one good stomp. A piece of wood from the doorjamb came away with the hardware of the door lock. Then Rex was inside, and Freddy thought, *Maybe I should run out the front.* That way he at least wouldn't get beat up. But then what if Rex decided to beat up Mom? Or the babies? He ducked down behind the back of the sofa so Rex couldn't see him. He noticed his hands kind of shaking. Maybe he could find some heavy thing and hit Rex with it. Or get Rex's gun. Did Rex still have that gun?

From behind the furniture the voices of the grown-ups were more muffled. "Good move, Rex," Mom was saying in a matter-of-fact kind of voice. "You broke my back door. What am I gonna tell the landlady?"

"Tell her your man is home. If you're still around to tell her anything."

"What's that supposed to mean?"

"They say you have another baby."

"Rex, I have a whole other life. You ain't in it. This ain't your home, I ain't your woman, and it ain't your baby."

"The next one'll be mine, anyways." There was a scuffling sound and a thud.

"Get your damned hands off me, Rex." Her voice sounded more desperate, kind of grunting and struggling.

"Maybe I don't feel like it." *Slap!* A heavy thump. Cursing, clattering, things falling on the floor.

I better go get Ralph, Freddy thought. He ran out the front way.

Bread and wine having been blessed, the churchgoers knelt at the rail to receive Communion. As they held out their hands, the sun broke through the clouds and came shining through the rose window. Mother Grey's sudden view of sunlight on the hands of the communicants was enchanting, one of those fleeting thrills that made the priesthood such a satisfying calling in spite of the difficulties and frustrations.

Then suddenly in the middle of Communion the front door to St. Bede's banged open and little Freddy appeared in a gust of frigid air, wearing no coat and no shoes. In his wet socks he ran up the aisle, vaulted the Communion rail, and dragged Ralph away by the sleeve of his cotta.

Nobody moved for a minute. Ralph looked like a great white moth flying out the front door. Some emergency with Saraleigh and the babies, no doubt; Mother Grey did not become alarmed right away. Her first thought was that Freddy should not be out without shoes and a coat.

Afterward, when she and Deedee had shaken the last hand and the two of them were tidying up, she said to Deedee, "I hope they're not in some kind of trouble."

"The Warthens?" said Deedee.

"No, not the Warthens. What makes you think anything's wrong with the Warthens?"

"The boy. He doesn't look well. I thought maybe he was on drugs or something."

"My word!"

"Wasn't he the one you saw reading the grimoire at the wedding?"

"Oh, Deedee, I don't think you ought to make too much out of that. He's a curious child, he probably just picked it up from Simon Ratcher's shelf of old books."

"And then he idly wrote the spells on a sticky."

"Children do strange things. It doesn't always mean anything."

"He doesn't look well to me," said Deedee. "There's a glow that healthy children have, and he's lost it."

"Edward is over here twice a week, taking religious instruction. I find him an apt pupil. I don't find him in the least unhealthy."

"I'm sorry. I hope I'm wrong. But I think you should consider the possibility that he's having problems."

Mother Grey agreed to consider that possibility. Meanwhile she called Saraleigh to be sure everything was all right and was told that this number was not in service. They must have neglected to pay the bill again. As she hung up the phone, she considered calling the number Dave had given her in Boston. She went so far as to dial the area code before changing her mind. She and Dave might need a long talk. The problems of Saraleigh and her brood were more pressing.

"I'm going over there to check on them," she told her friend. "Something must be wrong. That child shouldn't have been out in the snow in his stocking feet. I know it's hard to keep clothes on them sometimes, but this is ridiculous."

"I'll probably be gone by the time you get back," said Deedee. "I have to be in Ocean Prospect this afternoon. I'll ask Father Spelving if he knows anything about your grimoire; he's been studying Satanism lately in order to combat our local coven."

"Thanks."

Mother Grey changed out of her vestments and rushed over. No one answered Saraleigh's bell, so she went right up the back stairs. The kitchen was a scene of horrifying devastation. Chairs were broken, cooking pots and containers of food were scattered everywhere. There was a big stain on the floor that Mother Grey thought was blood, until she smelled the ketchup and saw the broken bottle. What could have happened here? She found Saraleigh sitting on the couch with her babies in her arms, puffing on a cigarette.

She had a monstrous black eye, swollen nearly shut.

"Saraleigh! My word, you look terrible! What happened to your eye?"

"Nothin' I can't handle."

"Don't tell me you and Ralph—!"

"No, honest. Nothin' like that. Don't worry about it. I'll be just fine."

"Have you seen a doctor?"

She ground her cigarette out. "Listen, I'm fine. I just need some money for a locksmith. Can you spare any? My door's broke."

"Yes, I saw."

"Also my pocketbook is gone."

"Your pocketbook?"

Ralph came in the front door, still in his cassock and cotta. "He got away," he said, and seeing Mother Grey, "Oh. Hi, Mother Vinnie."

"What's going on?" said Mother Grey. "Where is Freddy?"

"In the tub," said Saraleigh. "I made him take a hot shower after he ran all over town in the snow with no shoes on. Stupid kid." She lit another cigarette and began to cry, wiping her eyes on the back of her hand. Mascara got all over her face.

"I wish you would tell me what happened." Mother Grey hated guessing games. This was like some unpleasant charade.

Ralph and Saraleigh exchanged a despairing look. Then both began to speak at once, and stopped, and were silent for a beat, and then Ralph said, "Rex was here."

"He's got his old gun back," said Saraleigh. "He told me just as soon as he got some money, he was going to come and take me away."

"Got his gun back!"

"He took my pocketbook."

"We'll call Jack Kreevitch," said Mother Grey.

"Ha. Good luck on that."

"What's wrong with Jack?"

"Go on and call him, Mother Vinnie. See what he says. Just watch how Jack Kreevitch sees my side of this."

"We'll call nine-one-one, then. Maybe one of the others will be on duty."

The 911 dispatcher sent Kreevitch right over. Saraleigh reported that Rex had broken in, torn up the place, and attacked her. Sure enough, he seemed somewhat reluctant to go after him. "You want me to arrest Rex? I'm sure he's left town, Saraleigh."

"I don't care, Jack. You find him. Find him and jail his ass."

"Sure, and then tomorrow you'll tell me leave him alone, you love him, it was all a mistake. Meanwhile I gotta chase all over town looking for him, fill out all these papers and show up in court."

"Jack—!" Mother Grey protested.

"Well, that's what the two of them used to do all the time, Mother Vinnie. You weren't around then. I spent five years in and out of court with these two, back and forth to jail."

"That was when I didn't have nobody else," said Saraleigh.

"Right," he said. "Now you have Ralph. Well, why don't you get Ralph to take care of him?"

"Jack, for heaven's sake!" said Mother Grey.

"What I want to know is, is she going to file charges, Mother Vinnie," said Kreevitch.

"Fuckin' A I'm going to file charges!"

"Because I've been through this with her a million times."

"Jack, Ralph can't take care of this. Rex Perskie has a gun. This is a serious matter, and Rex has to be brought to justice." Ralph sat down on the floor in the corner, folded his hands in his lap, and began to bang his head against the wall, slowly and rhythmically.

"His gun isn't even loaded," said Kreevitch.

"How do you know that?" asked Mother Grey.

"Rex is a convicted felon," Kreevitch said. "Where would he get bullets?"

"Where did he get the gun?" said Saraleigh.

Mother Grey was astonished to see that Kreevitch was blushing. "It's not that I don't want to take care of it," he said. "It's just—I'm sure Brother Rex is out of town by now." Saraleigh shook her head slowly from side to side. "I mean, he has no place to stay."

"He stole my keys," said Saraleigh. "He probably thinks he's gonna stay here. You know, he told me he was gonna kill Ralphie."

"You'd better bring the children and move in with me for a few days until they get Rex locked up," said Mother Grey. "Ralph can bunk over at the halfway house till Saturday."

"Rex has your keys?" Kreevitch said.

Saraleigh put the sleeping baby down on the table and turned to Kreevitch. "Let me draw you a picture, Jack. Rex broke into my house, he beat me up and tried to rape me, he took all my keys and my money—that's the keys to the church, too, Mother Vinnie—and he said he would come back and get me as soon as he had enough dough to take me out of town."

Ralph's head-banging was becoming harder, the tempo faster. "Stop that, Ralph," Mother Grey said. He stopped.

"Well, okay," said Kreevitch. "We'll put out an APB on him. Come on, Saraleigh. I have to take you to the emergency room now."

"For what?"

"You're filing charges, right?" he said.

"It'll be all right," said Mother Grey. "Go with Jack and do what he says. Ralph and I will take care of the children and pack you some things. But don't come back here. After you're through at the hospital, go to my place. If I'm not home, the key is under the rock."

5

Saraleigh and Kreevitch left for the medical center. Ralph, meanwhile, was scratching himself, trembling, muttering things under his breath. The first thing Mother Grey did was find his medication—it was on top of the refrigerator, where the babies couldn't reach it— and make him take it. Then she hustled Freddy out of the tub and got him to dry and dress himself. After that, she threw some clothes and baby things from Saraleigh's bureau into a shopping bag. When it was full, she picked up the little plastic men scattered on the couch, in case Freddy might like to have something to play with at her house. They had jointed elbows and knees and fierce terrible expressions—those that weren't wearing menacing masks. Most were dressed in camouflage-colored outfits with Day-Glo accents. Some carried tiny little assault weapons. "War toys," she said.

"Sorry, Mother Vinnie," said Freddy, appearing fully dressed from his room. "I know you don't like me to play with war toys, but those are G.I. Joes. They're cool. They fight against enemies of the environment."

"I see," she said. "But I want you to be sure and remember that even against enemies of the environment, violence is not the answer, and guns are not cool."

"No, ma'am. Can I have them back?"

"Yes," she said, and gave them to him. Nasty little things.

Before they could go outside, Britney had to be stuffed into her snowsuit and baby Vinnie had to be changed and wrapped up in her winter bunting. Readying little ones to face the elements was a huge chore. *Something to think about,* Mother Grey reflected, *before St. Bede's day-care center opens.* In a matter of days she and her new staff might find themselves spending all their waking hours zipping up snowsuits, putting on boots, finding mittens, changing diapers. She noticed that Ralph still sat on the floor in the corner.

"You'd better pack some things for yourself, Ralph," she said.

"You don't think I should stay here and take care of Rex when he comes?"

"No, dear, I don't want you to get shot."

"You want me to go back to the group home."

83

"Don't you think it would be a good idea? Just till the end of the week. If you stay out of trouble and keep your job till the end of the week, you know, you get your health insurance. Then you and Saraleigh can go ahead and get married on Saturday."

He was silent for a long time, and then he said, "Okay."

"Come on, now." He got up and stuffed some clean underwear into his backpack.

They were all on their way out the back door when Mother Grey noticed that Freddy wasn't wearing his coat. She sent him back for it. He whined and protested: "It's warm, Mother Vinnie. It's above freezing. Look, it's thirty-five."

"It's wintertime, Freddy. Wear your coat." The ice-glaze that had encased the twigs of the trees was melting away, falling off sometimes and splattering on the sidewalk or making holes in the mushy snow. Still the cold was penetrating.

The snow, the texture of good sherbet, was excellent for packing. All the way to the group home, Freddy threw snowballs at the traffic signs. When he hit a sign, it went *clang* in a loud and satisfying way, and afterward the snow stuck to the painted metal surface for a moment before it slid down.

Ralph did not participate in these jollities. He was very low in his mind. He parted from them with what the psychologists like to call a flat affect and disappeared into the black hole of the young men's group home.

Mother Grey took the children to the rectory.

It was only a few blocks, but by the time she got home, she was frozen and exhausted. Britney could hold her hand and walk sometimes, but at other times the snow was too deep and she whined to be picked up. Mother Grey carried her on one hip while Baby Vinnie rode draped over her other shoulder.

Saraleigh hadn't arrived at the rectory from the medical center yet. Everyone was hungry. The little girls began to bawl. She left them crying on the living-room floor while she went to answer the telephone in the kitchen, closing the door to muffle the sound.

It was Dave Dogg calling. It was good to hear his voice. She began to burble the latest news at him, but he interrupted. "I need to talk to you, Vinnie," he said. He sounded confused and miserable.

"What's up?"

"Felicia wants me back."

So it was true, then. "What do *you* want, Dave?"

He didn't answer but sighed a long sigh. "It's strange, you know?" he said. "It just seems strange. We haven't been together in a long, long time. We aren't even the same people."

"Are you sure this isn't just because her mother is gone?"

"Maybe. I dunno." He said nothing more for what seemed like hours. She could hear him breathing. "What should I do?" he said at last.

This was very unfair. "Don't ask me to advise

you," she said. "I'm not a disinterested party. You aren't one of my clients. This is your decision. Make a list of the pros and cons. On the one hand, you and Felicia have your son. On the other hand, frankly, I have come to count on your being around. For what it's worth, I'm probably in love with you. I can't advise you." What could she say to him? "Flip a coin."

"Sorry," he said. "That was stupid."

"Don't worry about it."

In the background she heard the voice of Felicia herself, more irritating than New Age music, calling his name. "I gotta go," Dave said.

"'Bye, Dave," she said.

"Rex Perskie." Charlie Miller of Miller's Marine and Sporting Goods remembered all his customers, even from years back, and always greeted them by name. He hadn't seen much of Rex Perskie since he left the police force; somebody told him a while back he moved out of town or something. "Long time no see," he said. "Been away?"

"Yeah, Charlie," said Perskie. "I was away, but now I'm back. Got any thirty-eight wad cutters?"

Charlie reached into the safe, which stood open behind the cash register. "Gonna do some target practice?" he asked. Wad cutters—flat-pointed lead bullets with no jackets—were the ammunition of choice for target shooting and dry runs of one sort or another. They were cheap but effective, making a big round hole in the paper FBI target where your jacketed hollow-point bullet would leave a little cross. Police officers liked the jacketed hollow-points in dangerous situations for their stopping power. They would mushroom on impact. If you shot somebody with a wad cutter, it would just travel right on through. But wad cutters were good for target practice.

"Yeah, I thought I'd brush up on my skills," Perskie said. "Let me have two boxes."

Of course, Perskie wasn't a police officer anymore. There was something else about him that Charlie Miller was trying to remember. "Gotta check your driver's license," said Miller. "You know the rules." He took the two boxes of ammunition out of the safe.

"Right. Here it is." Perskie gave him his license, maroon and gray with big print. Good for three years, it expired in another month.

"Thanks," he said. "And sign the book right here."

Perskie took the pen to sign the book. Suddenly Miller remembered: Rex Perskie had been away doing time in jail.

He put the bullets back and kicked the safe door shut. "I can't sell you ammunition, buddy," he said. "You were convicted of a felony, right?"

"Where'd you hear that?" said Perskie.

"I heard it, is all. I can't sell you ammunition or guns. I'd lose my license."

"I ain't gonna do nothin'."

"That's not the point. I'm required by law not

87

to sell you any. Now, if you want some good fishing tackle or an outboard motor—"

"Shit," said Perskie. He turned on his heel and walked out.

Ralph, meanwhile, was dragging his sleeping bag out of the back of the halfway house's hall closet and preparing to make himself as comfortable as possible given the weight of his troubles.

"Frank had an episode last week and they took him back to the hospital. You can have his bed," said Danny.

"No thanks," said Ralph. "Last time I used Frank's bed, I got crabs."

"We could change the sheets."

"It's okay."

The halfway house was kind of dirty. Danny had written "wash me" and "dust me" on many of the available surfaces, as a reminder to himself, he said, but he seldom followed up. Bad smells. Whiskers in the bathroom sink, burnt stuff all over the kitchen stove. Paint flaking. It was like what you would expect with three guys living in a house.

"Your house is dirty," Ralph said.

"It needs a woman's touch. You ought to get Saraleigh over here again," Danny said.

"She won't come," Ralph said. "She doesn't want to clean your house."

"Schwartz is cooking tonight," Danny said.

"What's for dinner?"

"He doesn't know yet. He's pulling up some of the ten-minute recipes he keeps on the computer to see what looks good."

Sure enough, in fifteen minutes supper was on the kitchen table. Schwartz, frowzy-haired and gaunt, presided over the meal from the head of the table, an intense presence in thick glasses and camouflage cloth. He had selected pork and beans from his extensive list of ten-minute menus. The ingredients—canned pork and beans—were to be found in the basement pantry that Schwartz insisted on keeping stocked with a month's provisions in case of total social and economic collapse. He served their plates from the stove, reaching over with his long arms from where he sat.

"So, Ralph," said Schwartz, handing him a plate, "what is it this time? Not that I'm not happy to see you back or anything."

"Mother Grey told me to stay here tonight. There's this guy with a gun who wants to kill me."

"Schwartz, I really wish you'd include some green vegetables in your menus," said Danny. "You know, we're probably all going to get cancer from not eating our cruciferous greens."

"We can eat our cruciferous greens on your nights," said Schwartz. "Real men eat beans. Does the guy with the gun know you're here?"

"He'll probably guess. What am I going to do?"

"How the hell should we know?" snarled Schwartz, jabbing a piece of pork. "We're still crazy. You're the one who got out of the damned halfway house. You figure it out."

"I don't feel all that sane right now."

"How come?" said Schwartz.

"What if I can't go to work next week? I'll lose my health insurance, and then Saraleigh can't marry me." Welts were beginning to rise on the back of his right arm: the hives again. He scratched himself distractedly.

"If it weren't for the insurance industry, you wouldn't have this problem. Do you realize that?" said Schwartz. "Except for their lobbying efforts, we would have universal health insurance here like they do in Canada. You and Saraleigh and the children would all be covered, whether you were married or single, or had jobs, or were on welfare, or whatever."

"Really?"

"Really. What we really ought to do is go to Washington and assassinate Bob Dole."

"How would that help?"

"It would get rid of the Republicans."

"It would?"

"Sure. Cut off the head, and the body dies."

Danny rolled his eyes, and Ralph munched his beans in silence, trying to evaluate Schwartz's pronouncements. Sometimes the things he said made sense, but at other times his reasoning seemed flawed. Presently Schwartz spoke again. "Oh, by the way," he said, "nobody use the phone tonight."

"Why?"

"I have to get on the Internet and find something out for Mother Vinnie."

"What's that?" said Ralph.

"The Clavicles of Solomon."

"And what might the Clavicles of Solomon be?" Danny asked.

"That's the problem, isn't it? She doesn't know. She wants me to find out."

"So you're going to use the computer to go online to the Internet and tie up the phone again," Danny said.

"Right. If you have any calls to make, make them now."

"Thought I'd finish dinner first," said Danny.

"Feel free. Just remember."

And so as soon as dinner was over, Schwartz went into his room and closed the door.

Ever since Schwartz had found a discarded modem in a box of electronic garbage on Bridge Street, his life had changed. By putting it together with one of the XTs that Mother Grey had obtained for the halfway house from Rodman Sedgewick, he was able to communicate with distant strangers who had no idea he was supposed to be crazy. For a small fee, easily covered by his SSI check, the world was his.

He spent most evenings in his room, smoking cigars and hunching over the computer. That is, his physical body was there. His astral body was cruising through cyberspace, communing with lonely and (possibly) lovely women in dorm rooms and condominiums all over this glorious country of ours, or with real men who shared his interests in survivalism and martial arts.

There were several ways to gather information on the Internet. You could access one of the great informational databases, but connect time was expensive. Schwartz preferred to post queries to bulletin boards and round tables and then wait to see what replies people made. From the clues Mother Vinnie had given him, he surmised that any available information on the Clavicles of Solomon was to be found in the Satanism and Sorcery bulletin board, and so he checked in and identified himself. *Can anyone tell me anything about the Clavicles of Solomon?* he inquired. Then he noodled around among the messages already posted, to see what this bulletin board might be all about.

Many of the bulletin board messages were apparently announcements of meetings. With others, it was not so easy to tell what they were about by the name of the topic. He opened a message called *The Hand of Glory*, posted by someone calling himself Devil Boy. It proved to be a magic spell. You began, it said, with the severed hand of a hanged felon. Schwartz supposed he would have to hang his own felon, since in this day and age felons were no longer to be found dangling from every tree. Starting on the correct day of the week and the right phase of the moon, the sorcerer then put the hand through a number of disgusting procedures, with suitable incantations, until a little grease was obtained. This was used to make a candle, and the property of the candle was to immobilize anyone who saw its flame. *He calls this glory?* Schwartz thought. He had no use for it. Most of Schwartz's associates scarcely moved around at the best of times. What he really needed was a spell that would cause Danny to get busy and clean the house.

He closed the message and began to browse through a long series of messages that seemed to be a three-way philosophical argument among witches, or practitioners of Wicca, who called themselves old pagans and worshiped not Satan but Mother Earth; sorcerers, who sought to control demons but did not worship Satan either; and Satanists, who worshipped Satan and furthermore felt that it was appropriate to commit random acts of evil in order to please their master.

Toward the end of the discussion, one of the Wiccans posted a quote from *The Book of Ceremonial Magic* by Arthur Edward Waite, the same Arthur Edward Waite, she said, who had developed the popular Rider Tarot deck:

" . . . *the sorcerer of the Middle Ages was usually squalid and necessitous; hence he coveted treasures: he was usually despised, and hence he longed for mastery, for the prestige of mystery and the power of strange arts: he was usually lonely and libidinous, and hence he sought, by means of spells and philters, to compel the desire of women.*"

In other words, she said, *he was your basic nerd.*

At this, the sorcerers and Satanists told the Wiccans to get off the Satanist bulletin board and go form their own, with their crystals and their pagan holidays. Schwartz had to concur. Damned women. What did they know about squalor, necessity, loneliness, or libido? This whole crowd was giving him the creeps. He closed the message group and saw that a reply to his query had appeared on the board.

"The Clavicles or Keys of Solomon," said the message, *"are divided into the Greater and Lesser Keys. They are rituals that enable the performer to become master of a treasure possessed by spirits.*

"The Lesser Keys control the offices of all spirits at the will of the operator.

"The Greater Keys are powerful spells of black magic.

For more information, send me an e-mail."

It was signed by none other than Devil Boy himself.

Powerful spells, were they? Probably useful too. Spells like the Hand of Glory, where you first had to dismember a felon. He backed out of the round table and signed off, carefully printing the files he had saved to give to Mother Grey.

Then suddenly Schwartz realized that because he had signed on and identified himself, his name was now associated with Satanist cults in the records of the FBI, who undoubtedly monitored the Satanism round table. Even now his name and address were being forwarded electronically to the Fishersville police. Next, the boots on the stairway, the thundering knock on the door. But, no, nothing so overt. This was Fishersville, after all. Surveillance, though, certainly. They would be watching his every move from now on.

When Saraleigh walked in the door of the rectory, the howls of her babies, which had continued nonstop from the time that Mother Grey brought them home with her, ceased abruptly. It was one of those blessed miracles of sudden peace, like a breath of mountain air, or the moment when they stop running the paving breaker. For hours Mother Grey and Freddy had done their best to cheer his weeping sisters, but neither food, nor drink, nor toys, nor bottles of formula would stay the flow of tears. Mother Grey had even tried picking them up and bouncing them on her knee. They had made such painfully loud noises that she could scarcely stand being so close to them. Even Towser was affected by it and began to bark hysterically.

In order to run a day-care center, Mother Grey was going to have to hire staff. She had always known this, but this afternoon she fully experienced the truth of it. While the babies howled, she cracked the book again, the child-care center regulations of the State of New Jersey. There was quite a long bit about staff, how many advanced degrees were needed, how much experience. Clearly she needed to get busy and sort out the pile of résumés that had come trickling through the mail slot in response to her help-wanted ad.

Saraleigh walked in, took the children in her

arms, sat down, and lit up a cigarette. She appeared to be in a better frame of mind than when she left for the medical center with Officer Kreevitch to have her injuries examined. "It's all written down in the report now," she said. "Everything Rex did."

"Let's hope they can find him and bring him to justice," said Mother Grey.

"Yeah. Justice," said Saraleigh. "Jack's a good guy, but he and Rex are old buddies. Did you know that? They were best friends in grammar school."

Mother Grey did not know that. She knew they had been brother officers at one time, before Rex succumbed to alcoholism and had to leave the police force. But not grade school. Truly the roots of events in Fishersville went very deep. Once again Mother Grey felt like an outsider, a transient in this inbred old town. What did she know? How could she understand anything? She hadn't even gone to high school here.

"What's for dinner?" asked Saraleigh.

"Oh. Dinner. I hadn't even thought about it."

Saraleigh put down the babies, both of whom had fallen at once into an exhausted sleep. "Let me see what's in the kitchen," she said. "How about I make you some of my special beef stew?"

"Do we have enough beef?" said Mother Grey. For some reason, she was finding it difficult to get up out of her chair and see about the food.

"There's some. I'll put in lots of onions. Onions make it taste real meaty, onions and black pepper. Then if you put plenty of flour in the gravy, the meat goes a long way." She busied herself in the kitchen until good smells began to waft through the kitchen door.

When the stew was fairly cooking, she came out and sat on the couch next to the sleeping Britney. "I miss Ralphie," she said.

"I wish I could put you both up," said Mother Grey, "but if somebody like Father Bingley found out I encouraged unmarried couples to cohabit in the rectory, I could be in a lot of trouble."

"We wouldn't have to do nothin'."

"I meant stay together," said Mother Grey.

"If I was at my house, he would be sleeping on the sofa right now. That's what he does while I make dinner."

"It's just for a few days."

"He lays there in his underpants with one arm up over his head and snores."

"You like having him around," said Mother Grey.

"Ralphie's a good guy, you know? Comfortable. Not like Rex. When Rex used to sleep on the couch, it was like a time bomb. Everybody had to tiptoe, because if he woke up before he got sober, he started hitting."

"Do the children ever talk about him?"

"No. Britney don't even remember him. Jeez, I made a lot of stew. Are you sure we shouldn't get Ralph over here for dinner?"

"It would be hard for him to leave, don't you think?"

"I guess you're right." She sighed. "This time next week, we'll be married."

After they had dinner and did the dishes, Mother Grey retired to her room with a book, a scholarly work on abnormal adolescent psychology, as dense as it was depressing. The tendency to devil-worship was discussed at length. She put the book down. How well, actually, did she know little Edward? Could he fit this profile? Well, certainly. For all one knew, any given adolescent could fit any profile at all. They don't tell you much about themselves.

Not like grown men. *What I need is a good musical instrument,* she thought. There might not be a cello, but there was always the old Hook and Hastings tracker organ at St. Bede's. Maybe it could be played, just a little, for Saraleigh's wedding next Saturday. If she could find someone who did keyboard. She took a flashlight and went next door to inspect it.

The organ was a hundred years old, built into the side of the chancel, all paneled with oak. The pipes towered over her head. A brass plaque on the paneling declared that it was the gift of a Mr. John A. Kohl of Boston, Massachusetts, a former member of St. Bede's Parish, Fishersville, New Jersey. The plaque went on to say that the people of St. Bede's were indebted to Mr. Kohl for other large benefactions, aided by which they were enabled to erect and complete their new Church Edifice without debt, A.D. MDCCCXCII. *Those were the days*, thought Mother Grey.

In front of the keyboard was a simple oak bench at the right height for an organist to be able to reach all the banks of keys and the pedals as well. The old keys were covered with real ivory. The stops jutting out on either side of the keyboard were oaken knobs topped with circles of ivory, inscribed in elegant copperplate with the purpose of each stop: "4' Flauto Traverso Sw., 8' Stop'd Diapason, Sw. Super Octave Coupler." (Some knobs had no writing because the ivories had fallen off.) They looked almost like stoppers for decanters, or handles dispensing seltzer and sarsaparilla in a late Victorian soda shop.

All that ivory. How many elephants had given their lives for this organ? In vain, as it seemed; no one had played it in years. Mother Grey sat down and ran her fingers idly over the keyboard. The action of the keys was very stiff, and when she pressed them, they made clacking sounds. No music resulted; there was a motor that you had to start.

Mother Grey knew nothing about pipe organs, and not a whole lot about keyboard instruments generally. Strings were her forte. Perhaps the library could get her some books on tracker organ use and care from the interlibrary loan network.

There was an electrical switch by the keyboard. She turned it on and heard a faint hissing.

Good. The motor was still operating, anyway. She attempted a C major chord and was horrified at the results. Two of the notes made no sound at all. She played a few scales then, pulling different stops out, and found that the ratio generally was about the same: two more or less good notes, two silent. The organ needed a very great deal of work.

How much could she do herself? How, in fact, did a tracker organ work? Except for the keyboard and the pipes, the working parts were all hidden behind the oak paneling. Perhaps she should take the big flashlight for a critical look back there.

To the left of the keyboard was a loose panel, a small door maybe a foot and a half wide by a little more than five feet tall, smaller than a coffin lid. The panel had a keyhole at the top, but it was not locked. It was set into the wall without hinges. She lifted the panel off the wall and peered inside, not having to stoop, being not much over five feet tall herself.

There were more organ pipes inside rising up into the shadows, some of them plain square wooden things almost like long boxes, some of them fat cylinders, some tiny little pipes. They seemed to be connected to the keyboard by a system of wooden levers. Bits were hanging off of the mechanism here and there—old leather, perhaps.

At her feet the floor dropped down into darkness. She shined the flashlight down and saw that the drop was about three feet to a crude unfinished floor, dark gray with dust, and that steps led down to it. At the edge of the floor, a very narrow trapdoor could be seen. Proceeding downward, she began to notice the mouse droppings and then the mouse, quite mummified, the outline of its little ribs visible through the hair.

Suddenly her mind went back to the time she had stumbled over the dead body of the bishop in a dark, dusty cloakroom. *I can do this tomorrow*, she thought, *in the daylight*. She backed slowly toward the coffin-lid opening. *There's plenty of time*.

She was still inside the organ chamber when she heard a faint sound like the sound of the side door opening—a door that was always kept locked—and then the sound of someone coming into the church.

For an instant Mother Grey found herself paralyzed with terror. Then she told herself, *This is my church. No one is going to frighten me in my own church*. And if it came to that, she did have a heavy flashlight with her.

Slowly she put her head out of the hole in the organ. Nothing looked out of the ordinary. The light was on in the sanctuary, but the nave was so dark that not even the front pews were clearly visible. Was someone there? There was a creak, but the old church always creaked, all by itself.

There was definitely a draft. She came all the way out of the hole in the paneling and called out: "Is anyone there?" The play of the flashlight beam did less to illuminate the darkness than to pick out and distort shapes that the light fell on, making them into something scary. She went down the steps and shined the light into the side vestibule.

The door to the outside was open. In the flashlight beam she saw a man's hand.

The sight was so startling that she screamed, not a movie scream but a little shriek, sort of like

"Ow!" It was involuntary. She did not care to think of herself as the sort of woman who screamed. The hand was withdrawn at once, and the door banged.

Mother Grey turned on the lights, wasting electricity to light up a completely empty church. Then she went to the side door, holding the heavy flashlight like a weapon. *Imagine my hitting someone*, she thought. *What an idea*. The prowler was probably some backsliding member of the St. Bede's AA group, looking for something to steal; could she strike one of these lost sheep with a blunt instrument?

But what if he tries to hit me first?

The door was not latched. Had she forgotten to lock it? She opened and looked out, but the snowy streets offered no trace of the intruder.

Now, why had she shoveled that walk? If she hadn't shoveled the walk, she could have gotten Officer Jack Kreevitch to follow the man by his footprints and catch him. Maybe it was Rex Perskie himself! But no. What would he want in a church? More likely the man was some would-be worshiper coming in to say his prayers, who tried the door and found it unfastened. Then she had scared him away with screaming. *I'll call the police in the morning*, she decided, and carefully locked the door.

Back in the rectory, Saraleigh told her that Ellen Warthen had called.

"Said she had to talk to you. Said it was urgent. An emergency. Something awful happened, she said."

6

Mother Grey called the Warthens at once. The major answered, affable as ever. "Everything's fine," he said. "It was just a family matter. We're sorry to have disturbed you." Mother Grey bade him good night. Not until she hung up the phone did she remember the way he had behaved at the wedding.

"Saraleigh, what made you think it was an emergency?"

"That's what Mrs. Warthen said. She was mighty upset. Or maybe she's always like that, I dunno. Did you talk to her?"

"No, I talked to him."

"You should talk to her."

"He told me it was a family matter," said Mother Grey, and as she said it, she realized that in some circles that was a code phrase for "I'm beating my wife." Saraleigh knew it too; she raised one eyebrow.

What a horrifying idea. But it seemed so unlikely. Of course, to Saraleigh, victim of an abusive man, all men were potentially abusive. Mother Grey tried to picture the cool and genial Major Warthen flying into a passion and striking his wife. It didn't fit. He was rather the sort who would walk out if he was unhappy and go someplace where he would be happier. If anything, the traffic would be in the other direction: Ellen Warthen, maddened by her husband's unflappability, would go at him with the fire tongs in an effort to make some sort of impression.

Unless there actually was something between her and that odious antiques dealer.

Perhaps she'd better give them another call. Better still, she could drop in. It wasn't all that late. Then if there were bruises and blood . . . but this was ridiculous.

She put on her coat and boots.

Mother Grey approached the Warthens' house resolutely, concentrating on the places she was putting her feet one after the other, so as not to have to think of what might be there when the door was opened. One of her least favorite duties as a pastor was mediating in family disputes. No one—no group, that is, nor any particular sort of appearing person—was immune to domestic violence. She and Dave had talked about this sometimes. As a city homicide detective, he knew all the statistics on family murder and was also unpleasantly familiar with particular cases: how the body had looked when it was found, and all the rest of it.

Could that actually be what was going on with the Warthens? The wife, hysterical over the telephone, the husband insisting it was a family matter. Their front walk was shoveled and well salted. Of course, Major Warthen would have salted his walk, or insisted that his son carry out this duty. Whatever they might be, the Warthens were never slovenly.

Mother Grey raised the brass knocker and rapped at the door.

Murmuring voices sounded inside. Steps approached, and the door swung open.

"Mother Grey!" Ellen Warthen stood at the door in slacks and a sweater and no makeup, looking about half her age. She was pale and her eyes were rimmed with red, but she did not appear to have been beaten. Good. Yet there was an edge of hysteria to her voice as she tried to maintain the forms of politeness. "I *wish* I could ask you in," she said, "but it's *such* a bad time. I'm sure you understand."

I don't understand what it is that I'm supposed to understand. Wasps, who love peace and quiet and detest open conflict and drama, maintain their surface tranquillity by sending each other subtle cues to indicate what they need from one another, but years of life in New Jersey among a diversity of ethnic customs had blunted Mother

Grey's sensitivity to these cues. Dimly she perceived that Ellen Warthen wanted rather desperately for her to go away. Why? What was going on?

"Is there anything I can do?" she asked.

"No." Ellen Warthen seized her hand and squeezed it and patted it. "No. We can work this out ourselves. Good night, Mother Vinnie." Then she closed the door in her face.

As a general rule, most small-town police officers have more ammunition than they use, and they tend to keep it around the house. For a man willing to turn his back on law and order, there was always the possibility of stealing ammunition from an old brother officer. So it was that Rex Perskie went to Jack Kreevitch's place looking for bullets. He remembered that Kreevitch used to keep spare ammo in his gym bag. With five children in the house, Kreevitch would be sure to keep his gun locked up, but maybe not the gym bag.

Perskie staked out Kreevitch's house from the shelter of a toolshed in the yard across the street, smoking, drinking from a pint bottle of whiskey, and waiting for the last lights to go out. It was a little like deer-hunting, he reflected. You had to be able to stand the cold and inactivity.

As soon as he thought everyone was asleep, he crept around to the back. It was a clear moonlit night, and the snow made crunching sounds when he stepped on it, so he feared every moment to be discovered and challenged. But nobody came. For a couple of minutes he tinkered with the back-door lock. It would not open. Time for more brutal measures. Wrapping his jacket around his fist, he broke a pane of glass, reached in, and turned the knob.

The back door gave onto a laundry and mud room. Moonlight streamed in the window, glittered on the broken glass, and showed a row of winter jackets of every size hanging on pegs. On the last peg hung Kreevitch's gym bag. Perskie unzipped the bag and reached in. Bingo. As his fingers closed over the plastic box of bullets, it made a little rattling sound.

Then he heard another noise: dog toenails on the kitchen linoleum. *A dog? What was it doing while I was breaking in?* Kreevitch's dog must be stone deaf. Just the same, it could probably bite. He stuck the box of shells in his pocket and slipped out, pulling the door closed behind him. When the dog started barking, Perskie ran for it.

He knew of another unlocked shed down by the old railroad tracks. A three-block run got him there in no time. The accommodations were pretty comfy if you didn't mind the cold. Other homeless persons, gone now, who knew where, had dragged in a mouse-infested mattress and a couple of smoky, greasy blankets. With enough whisky, Perskie could make himself easy there all night long.

Snug among the blankets, he took a good swig of his whiskey and got out his revolver, admiring it by the faint light of the halogen streetlamp that shone through the dirty window. Slowly he took a few of Kreevitch's bullets and rolled them around in his palm, thinking of Saraleigh and her lover. *I ought to write their names on the casings.* That was a lot of trouble, though, and Perskie didn't really like to write. Anyway, he had nothing to write with. So he tried to load his gun.

It was then that he found that Kreevitch's bullets were made to fit the nine-millimeter semiautomatic that the police were carrying these days. He could not use them with his old revolver. *Shit.*

What he needed was some .357 Magnum shells, or even .38s. Now who the hell would have .38s? He drained the whisky from his hip flask, pulled the blankets up around his shoulders, and fell asleep considering the problem.

Light was pouring in the upstairs-hall window of the halfway house. Ralph awoke, unzipped his bag, and stretched. He hated sleeping bags. They were too tight to let him curl up, so that he always woke up with a sore back.

At least he had some chance of a decent breakfast, since it was Danny's turn to cook. Schwartz made them eat manly food—fried grease and C-rations or something like that. Was that the smell of coffee? He pulled on his jeans and crept down the back stairs.

The smells of coffee, eggs, maple syrup, and hot butter curled up from the kitchen and met his nose, mingled with the usual backstairs mildew and mouse smells. As he put his hand on the backstairs doorknob, Ralph realized that Danny and Schwartz were talking about him.

"The way I see it," Schwartz was saying, "Ralph has got to take this guy out."

Ralph paused to listen. The glass doorknob was cold in his hand.

"You mean kill him?" said Danny.

"How else is he going to get rid of him? The police won't do anything. They're too busy spying on innocent citizens like me."

"The police are spying on you? Why would they want to do that?"

"In any event. He has to kill him, and then get rid of his body some way so that it will never be found, or make it look like an accident."

"I don't know, Schwartz—"

Ralph turned the knob and stepped casually out of the back stairwell and into the kitchen, tucking his shirt into his pants. "So what's for breakfast?" he said.

"French toast," said Danny. "I made it out of Egg Beaters. Regular eggs have too much cholesterol."

"As long as there's syrup."

"Listen, Ralph, Dan and I have been discussing your problem."

"So I heard," said Ralph, helping himself to the rest of the French toast. It was too cold to melt the butter, so he put it in the microwave oven.

"What we decided is that you have to waste this guy," said Schwartz.

"What Schwartz decided," said Danny. "I think it would be very dangerous. If this person didn't get you before you got him, then you'd probably get caught by the police. Maybe even executed. They give you a shot for that nowadays, Ralph. You know how you hate needles."

"What a wussie you are, Dan," said Schwartz. "Ralph is defending his woman and his home. His duty in this matter is clear. Not a jury in the country would convict him. Look, man, we'll help you."

The microwave beeped. Ralph took his plate out and mixed syrup with the melted butter. He wondered how it was that his friends proposed to help him. After a couple of bites of French toast, he noticed that the hives were popping out on his neck now. "Have you guys seen my backpack? I think I need to take my medication."

A knock sounded at the back door. Schwartz jumped, spilling his coffee, and muttered, "Jesus, they're here already," as he wiped it up. But when they looked, it was nobody any more threatening than Freddy Kane. The top of his head with its little cowlick stuck up above the window frame.

"Come in, Fred," Ralph called. The boy rattled the knob. Schwartz had to get up and unlock the door first.

"Why is the door locked?" said Freddy. He stamped the snow off his feet and took off his coat.

"I'm expecting trouble," Schwartz told him.

"Cool underwear," Freddy said. Schwartz's

undershirt and boxers were printed in the Desert Storm camouflage pattern. Schwartz acknowledged the compliment with a nod.

"I just wanted to tell you I been watching our apartment," said Freddy, "in case Rex comes back. Is there any more of that?"

"I can make you some," said Danny. He opened another box of Egg Beaters and dumped the contents into a bowl.

"I thought the police were watching the apartment," Ralph said.

"Jack Kreevitch comes around sometimes, but nobody's really staking it out. Except me."

"Aren't you kind of young to tangle with grown men?" Danny said. He dipped bread into the egg mixture and dropped the slices, sizzling, into a hot buttered pan.

"I ain't gonna tangle with him," said the boy. "I'm gonna call you guys, and you can come and tangle with him."

"Good," said Schwartz.

"You're gonna kill him, right, Ralph?" Freddy said. "You have to. Right? I mean, he hurt my mom."

Danny said, "Oh, come on, Fred. You're talking about your dad. You don't really want Ralph to murder him." He put a plateful of French toast on the table.

"He ain't either my dad. He's Britney's dad." Freddy took the plastic syrup bottle and directed a stream of lite syrup at the stack of French toast. "I guess he's my stepdad."

"I thought I was your stepdad," said Ralph. The itching was getting worse.

"Yeah, sure, Ralph, you're my stepdad. Rex must be my ex-stepdad. Anyway, you have to kill him. Don't tell me you're not going to do it." The French toast was soaked with syrup. Freddy proceeded to cut it up into small neat squares, his thin elbows wagging in the air.

"Why don't you just go and get the police when he comes around?" Danny asked.

"The police love him," said Freddy with his mouth full. "They wouldn't do nothin'. Jack Kreevitch and him are best friends." He swallowed the last bite and jumped up. "I gotta go. I'll come back and get you when he comes around."

"Don't forget your coat," said Danny. "It's cold out."

"Oh. Right." He put his coat back on and rushed out the door.

Schwartz and Danny were looking at Ralph, waiting for his next move. He took a deep breath. It seemed that they all expected him to be a man and perform violent manly acts. He pushed himself away from the table and stood up. "So I'm supposed to kill him," he said.

"I don't think so, Ralph. I think you'd better call the police," said Danny.

Schwartz glared at him. "Leave him alone," he said. "Ralph will do the right thing."

"I haven't ever killed anybody before," said Ralph. "I wasn't in the service or anything. I don't know if I can do this."

112

"It's like anything else, Ralph," said Schwartz. "You go over it a couple of times in your mind, maybe you practice some moves, and then you'll be ready."

"Go over it?"

Danny gave a snort of contempt and began to clear away the breakfast dishes. Schwartz said, "You know, rehearse it. How do you want to do this? Like, here I am, I'm Rex coming at you with a gun. Now, what do you do?"

"I dunno." Ralph's hands felt large and heavy. "Isn't he gonna shoot me if I try anything?"

Whatever it was that Schwartz muttered was lost in the noise of the water Danny was running into the dishpan. "Come on," said Schwartz. "I can see we're going to have to have a little martial-arts training session here." He dragged Ralph into the living room and cleared a space in the middle of the rug.

"Okay, I'm you," he said. "Obviously you're going to need some kind of weapon, since your adversary is armed." He pulled a baseball bat from the umbrella stand. "This will do okay. Now, you be Rex and come at me with a gun."

"No," said Ralph.

"What's the matter?"

"You'll hurt me."

"No, I won't. I promise I won't hurt you."

But he had that mad light in his eye, and Ralph didn't trust him. "Here," said Ralph, offering the coat tree. "This is Rex. He's coming at me with a gun. You're me." He stepped aside to view the correct moves as performed by Schwartz.

"First of all, you have to focus your mind," said Schwartz. "This is your worst enemy. He wants to kill you. He defiled your woman. You can never be happy while this man lives. Got it?"

"Are you gonna show me anything or not?" said Ralph. All this talk was making him uncomfortable.

"You want moves," said Schwartz.

"Yes."

"Okay." Schwartz stood for a long moment contemplating the coat tree, about three yards away from it. Suddenly he inhaled sharply and stepped into range of its imaginary arms, swinging the bat upward and to his left as if to disable a gun hand. Almost in the same motion, he brought the bat around and struck the top of the coat tree a terrific wallop. It toppled over, the coats and hats flying. When the blow connected, Schwartz seemed to change; hitting the coat tree released some monster inside him. His face twisted with rage, and he hit it again and again, cursing, bringing the bat up and down on it like an ax.

It made a thundering great racket. Splinters flew; the coats were in tatters; the coat tree itself cracked in two.

"There," said Schwartz, drawing himself erect, straightening the glasses on his face. He took in a breath and let it out sharply. His calm demeanor was back. "That's how it's done. Think you can handle it?"

Down in the cellar of the Umbrella Works, Simon Ratcher was busy dismantling the chapel and hiding the pictures of his boys. The pictures would go into an envelope to be mailed to himself, the accoutrements of the chapel into a hidey-hole behind a secret panel. He should have done this earlier, but he didn't think of it until this morning; the police would be coming here as soon as he called them to report that he'd killed a burglar. Once they arrived, he couldn't very well tell them to stay away from the cellar. That wouldn't be reasonable.

Luckily it was Monday, the day the Umbrella Works was closed, so that not only was he able to do the cleanup work without interruption, he was able to look forward to an afternoon nap. He would need it. All through the night he had sat in front of the fireplace, waiting, dozing intermittently, his shotgun trained on the French windows. When the burglar showed his nose, Ratcher's plan had been to blow his head off, salt the crucifix away in the secret hiding place, and put everything else in a pillowcase in the ex-con's lifeless hand. The photo he wanted would still be in the man's pocket, of course. Where else would he have left it? He had nowhere to stay in town.

But the night passed, and the ex-con never showed.

If he didn't get here by midday, Ratcher would have to go back to his apartment without concluding their business, if only to feed the cat. If he then came while Ratcher was away from the Umbrella Works, there would have to be an alternate plan. *I'll do whatever's necessary,* Ratcher assured himself.

He was beginning to wonder what was keeping the fellow.

Monday, the day when such upscale antiques and collectibles stores as the Umbrella Works were closed, was the one day when Charpentier's Flea Market was open. From all over the Delaware Valley in foul weather and fair, even in the dead of winter, dealers arrived before dawn to set up their tables, and all morning long their customers came flocking.

Today there was quite a crowd, in spite of the slushy mud underfoot and the scudding clouds overhead. Here many things were for sale at deep discounts, children's clothing, spices, Mexican silver jewelry, pots and pans. A young Peruvian woman with a thick black plait down her back sold heavy sweaters, brown and gray, that smelled of sheep. Across the aisle from her table was a booth where Nazi memorabilia was offered for sale, along with old coins and the occasional block of stamps.

Rex Perskie knew the man who ran this booth, a mouth-breather with long hair and pimples. He was deep into survivalism, and for survival you need firearms. The guns and ammo were not kept on top of the table; in fact, they were in the trunk of his car. He would show them to you only if he knew you.

"Rex! How's it hangin'? Ain't seen you in a while."

"Can't complain," said Perskie. "Got any three-fifty-seven Magnum slugs?"

"Some hollow-points. How many you need?"

"A box."

"No problem," said the survivalist. Perskie paid him for them and slipped them in his pocket. Now all that remained was the cold hike back to Fishersville.

The same clouds that scudded across the skies of Charpentier's Flea Market darkened St. Bede's as Mother Grey went to the church to begin making preparations for Ash Wednesday, which would be day after tomorrow. She was pleased to see that the snow was all gone from the south side of the steep slate roof, that it had apparently slid off without injuring anyone or crushing anything valuable. Warmed by the intermittent sun, the dark roof was gently steaming, even with the thermostat set down. (It *was* set down, wasn't it? She must check and make sure.) Perhaps there would be no more snow this year.

Ash Wednesday, the beginning of the Lenten season of penitence and reexamination, the first true harbinger of spring, was a time greatly to be welcomed, of spiritual cleansing and reduced oil bills. Mother Grey let herself into the sacristy with a laundry list of chores in her pocket (one of which was actually the laundry). Mentally she added the chore of checking the thermostat. But as soon as she closed the door behind her, all the chores flew right out of her mind.

Something in the old church was not as it should be.

There was a cold draft in her face that shouldn't have been there. Not if the doors and windows were all securely fastened. There was also a faint smell of a man needing a bath, unwashed hair, unwashed armpits. Was someone in the church?

She took another step inside. It was cold, it smelled of mice. Maybe she had imagined the man smell. She eyed the ceiling and noticed a leak streaking down the plaster and raising the grain on the oak paneling. Then she saw water stains on the carpet that weren't under any leak. Melting snow. Salty mud stains. And something, a door or a window, was definitely open.

Was someone in the church?

She went to the side door where the man had come in the night before. The lock had been forced, and the door stood ajar. Any number of murderous felons could be hiding behind the pews.

"Is anyone here?" she called. There was no answer, naturally; murderous felons seldom declare

118

themselves. Mother Grey was getting the creeps. Just in case there was any real danger, she put her hand out for the processional crucifix. In a pinch it would do as a defensive weapon.

It wasn't where she had left it.

Burglars had been in St. Bede's.

What else had they taken? More than a few things. She thought, *I'll have to make a list, which means I'll have to remember everything that was here before.* She didn't hear movements or anyone breathing. Probably the burglars were gone.

It was hard to think straight. Using the phone in the sacristy, putting her back to the wall in case of attack, she called 911 and reported the burglary. Then she got a pencil and paper and cautiously went back to the chancel to list everything that was missing.

First of all, the processional crucifix was gone from its place in the corner. After that, the silver Communion chalice that Belle-Mère had given her when she was ordained. *This town is hard on heirlooms,* she thought. Fortunately she was a woman of few possessions. Except the more she thought of herself as a woman of few possessions, the more things turned up missing that she was unhappy to lose. Maybe she was fooling herself about her detachment from the material world.

Simon Ratcher, the fellow who gave demonic books to young boys, had wanted that crucifix. How badly? Could he have broken in here and taken it? But no; he smelled like sandalwood. (But

119

that would be when he was trying. Maybe in his natural state he smelled like an unwashed man.)

She should have called the police last night. The man she frightened away must have come back.

Where was her good black cassock?

"I seen him, Ralph!" Freddy hung in the kitchen doorway of the halfway house, panting. "I seen him!"

Ralph looked up from his second breakfast. "Was he hanging around the apartment?"

"No, he, like, walked past. But I followed him and found out where he went."

Ralph sighed deeply and pushed himself away from the table.

"Okay, where did he go?"

"The umbrella factory. Probably he'll be there awhile," the boy said. "He went in the back way. I can show you where."

7

After all his preparations, after preparing the premises of the Umbrella Works so that a close inspection by police officers would reveal nothing that could reflect badly on himself, after cleaning, oiling, and loading the shotgun, Simon Ratcher was taken unawares.

The ex-con, not so tame as it turned out, walked in the back door of the Umbrella Works with the bag of church loot over his left shoulder and a .357 Magnum in his right hand.

"Why the gun, friend?" Ratcher said to him. "This is a friendly business transaction. Isn't it?"

The bag was a black cassock, actually. The ex-con had stuffed it with stolen artifacts and tied it at the bottom. The handle of the processional crucifix was sticking out the end. He untied the bag, pulled out the crucifix, and shook the rest of the contents out onto the counter.

"Here's the stuff," he said. "Give me the money."

"There was, I believe, a photograph?" said Ratcher.

The ex-con pulled it from his pocket and tweaked it between his fingers. "The money first," he said. "Then you get the photograph."

"I don't have that much on me."

"Try the safe in your office."

"Oh, maybe there's something here—" He reached under the counter for the shotgun, only to hear a click as the ex-con pulled back the hammer of the revolver.

"Don't try it," the ex-con said. "I know where your safe is. Get in there."

"No need to be rude," said Ratcher.

"Shut up and get me the money."

"Of course. Step right this way." They went into the office. The ex-con stood over him, glowering, as he opened the safe. "I hope there's enough in here," said Ratcher.

"Give me the money, you stupid fucker. Give it to me now, or you're dead."

Scarcely ten minutes passed from the time when Mother Grey dialed 911 to the time when Jack Kreevitch and Officer Jimmy Finn arrived at St. Bede's. Jack filled out the necessary report while Officer Finn prowled around the church, looking for evidence or maybe for concealed burglars. The report called for the silliest information. "Jack, you know perfectly well that I'm thirty-seven," said Mother Grey. "But what earthly difference does my age make?"

"Have to put it down," he said.

She gave him the list of missing objects, her best guess anyway. "I'll let you know if anything else turns up missing," she said.

"I hate to see this kind of thing in Fishersville," Kreevitch said, shaking his head from side to side. "First the library, and now this."

"The library? Was the library robbed?"

"Somebody broke in and took that bronze bust that used to be on the check-out desk."

"Is it a crime wave, then?"

"Almost looks that way. Don't tell the *Clarion*."

"The *Clarion* wouldn't let on, even if I did tell them. They only print good news."

"Last B and E we had before that was the guy who used to get in and take the women's purses when they left 'em in sight of the first-floor windows."

"Did you ever catch him?"

"No, but we got a good description. If he ever shows up in town again, his butt is mine."

"Maybe this is him again."

"Don't think so. Different MO."

"Tell me something, Jack. Doesn't this strike you as strange? Burglarizing a poverty-stricken church. What's the point?"

"We've heard of a number of break-ins of

small churches around the state. Only the silver taken, usually."

"What for? Silver is practically worthless these days."

"There's one theory that these things are being shipped to South America, to churches there."

Mother Grey wondered what sort of priest would want to serve Communion from a hot chalice. But something else was at work here. "Jack, I think Simon Ratcher might be behind this particular burglary. He asked me to sell him our processional crucifix the other day, and I refused."

"Yo, Jack, look at this," Officer Finn called out. By the door he had found a wet, sandy, salty footprint, not really big, maybe a man's size nine. Not a sneaker print, either, with its patterns and identifying marks, but a perfectly featureless sole and heel. That in itself was unusual; most men in Fishersville wore athletic shoes.

The latent detective slumbering within Jack Kreevitch was fully awake now, roused by the finding of an actual clue. "Put a ruler next to that footprint, and take a picture of it, Jimmy," he said to the other man.

"I didn't bring no ruler," Finn protested, "and I didn't bring no camera, either."

"Go back to the station and get 'em. It's only a block away." Grumbling, Finn set off for the station in the basement of City Hall to get the necessary tools.

Kreevitch began to examine the floor with keen interest. "Our friend went out this way," he said, following the marks on the floor out the side portal. Mother Grey followed him, pulling her coat tight against the cold. "If it was only one guy, maybe he couldn't carry all that much," he was muttering. "Maybe he stashed it."

"You think our things might still be here somewhere?"

"It's worth a look," he said. He walked all around the church, looking in the window wells and behind the bushes. Mother Grey followed him. The wind sighed in the bare tree branches.

Suddenly a rumbling noise sounded over their heads, and the snow slid off the north side of the roof of St. Bede's, falling with a crash right in front of them. The way they both jumped, it might have been a dead body.

"Be careful where you step," said Mother Grey. The policeman gave her a sour look. "There might be footprints," she said. "You wouldn't want to step on them, Jack. It would confuse the evidence."

"I've been doing this for fifteen years," he said. "Don't worry about me." He was looking very carefully at the ground. Except for what had fallen from the roof, the crust of the snow on the north side was unbroken.

Suddenly Kreevitch's eye fell upon Rodman Sedgewick's freezer. Like everything else in town, the freezer had been coated in the night with a skin of ice. Still, the ice was cracked in places, and the snow around the freezer, melted and scuffed.

It might be that the freezer had been opened quite recently. And yet. Wasn't it locked?

Kreevitch glared at the freezer with disapproval. "You know, this is a bad thing to have around, Mother Vinnie. A kid could get into it and smother."

"I know, Jack," she said. "This afternoon. I'll do something about it this afternoon. But it's locked, you know. Nobody can get into it without the key."

"Even if you just block the door somehow so that it won't close all the way."

"Jack, it's perfectly safe. It won't open."

"Anything in it?"

"No, it's empty."

"I'd like to take a look in it just the same."

"I think it's empty." Maybe it wasn't. Actually she never had gotten a chance to look inside the damned thing, what with the frantic pace of life at St. Bede's these days. She produced the key, and Kreevitch fitted it into the lock, scraping the ice out first.

"Let's see what we've got here." He opened the lid. A thin, flat piece of ice slid off and shattered on the ground. He looked inside.

"Christ on a crutch," he said softly.

A dead child? The loot? What? She rushed over, heedless of the footprints she might be obliterating, and gazed for the first time into the freezer that Rodman Sedgewick had given her.

Fifteen dead cats were piled inside, stiff as boards.

"Satanists," she said.

"What?"

"This has to be the work of the Satanists. Dee-dee told me I'd know it when I saw it, and I do."

"Okay, but does it have anything to do with the burglary here?"

"I don't know. How could it? The freezer was locked the whole time. Unless there's another key."

"Where did this freezer come from?"

"Rodman Sedgewick."

"The senatorial candidate? Gave you a freezer full of dead cats? That would look great in *The Trentonian*, wouldn't it?" He began to laugh.

"Maybe I'd better call him."

"Call him."

They went back inside, and she dialed Sedgewick's number. It was busy.

"You know," said Kreevitch, "this reminds me of a story I heard about a Chinese restaurant that burned down in South Jersey." He was still chuckling.

"Jack, I have a very strong feeling that we'll find the proceeds of this burglary at the Umbrella Works, if we act quickly enough."

"The only thing that wasn't burned up in this fire was the freezer. When they opened it, what do you think they found?"

"Of course, if you wait long enough, Simon Ratcher will have time to get my things out of town, off on their way to South America," she said.

"They found a whole bunch of dead cats."

"Jack, this isn't about oriental cuisine. It's about Satanist rituals."

"At the Umbrella Works?"

"Does it seem so far-fetched?"

"Not really. As a matter of fact, we've been watching Simon Ratcher's place. Kids go there, teenagers and even younger, stay in there a long time."

"What do they do?"

He shrugged. "I don't think it's a Bible study group."

"My word! What are you going to do?"

"Tough to do anything. You have to find out what's going on that's against the law, and then you have to prove it. Takes time."

"If we go over there right now, we might catch Simon Ratcher with the proceeds of this burglary. You could put him in jail for that, couldn't you?"

The policeman sighed. "If we want to search the Umbrella Works, I'll have to get a warrant," he said.

Ralph walked slowly down the street, letting the big end of the baseball bat trail in the snow.

Between the Umbrella Works and the river was a flagstone terrace surrounded by evergreen bushes. There were statues on the terrace, bare-naked ladies with lumps of snow melting on their shoulders and breasts, some of them trying to cover themselves with towels, little boys peeing in fountains, soldiers on horseback, angels from some Catholic cemetery. The surface of the flagstones was covered with melting ice. Ralph pushed past the bushes and nearly slipped and fell.

Rex Perskie was coming out of the back door to the factory. He looked at Ralph with surprise and hostility but said nothing.

"I came to tell you something, Perskie," said Ralph.

"What?"

"Stay away from Saraleigh."

"What if I don't friggin' feel like it?"

Ralph sighed. *You defiled my woman. I can never be happy while you live.* He took a couple of steps closer, until he was about three yards away. He was ready now, but he was still hoping not to have to do it. "Get out of town," he said. "Leave now. Don't come back."

"Fuck you," said Perskie. He reached into the back waistband of his trousers and pulled his gun.

Not until later did Ralph think, *What if he turned out to be left-handed? Or what if he wasn't the right height?* As it was, the moves Schwartz had shown him worked perfectly. Perskie's arm broke with a satisfying *crack!* The gun went flying out of his hand and over the bushes. The bat connected with his head on the return stroke so neatly and swiftly that he fell to the ground even before he was able to curse.

It was almost an anticlimax. He just lay there. Ralph stood looking at him for a long time, feeling relieved not to have gone berserk like Schwartz and beaten his fallen adversary to a bloody pulp. *But Schwartz is crazy,* he thought, not for the first time. *And I'm not.*

So why did I take his advice?

There was a rustling in the bushes. Freddy came through, followed by Schwartz and Danny.

"How did it go?" asked Schwartz.

"He's dead," said Ralph.

"How do you know?" said Freddy.

"Look at him," said Ralph. The body was stretched out in the snow, not moving. A little puddle of blood had formed beside Rex's gray face.

Freddy scratched his head. "I seen him look like that lots of times."

"What am I going to do?" Ralph whispered, almost to himself.

"We'll fix it, Ralph. Leave it to us," said Schwartz.

"You did the right thing, Ralph," said Danny. "Just go tell Saraleigh he left town or something, and we'll do the rest."

"You'll take care of it?" Ralph said.

"Sure. We can handle the situation. Go home. Here, Dan, you take his feet. Freddy, you get Ralph's bat and come with us."

As he pushed his way out through the bushes, Ralph glanced over his shoulder once to see his friends struggling with the body. It almost seemed as though Schwartz was going through the pockets. But no; he must have been getting a better grip. Freddy was picking something up from the ground—the baseball bat, probably. They were handling the situation. He could leave it to them. He sighed, then hurried away in the direction of St. Bede's rectory to get Saraleigh and the babies. It was okay for them all to go home now.

He hadn't gone but a half a block when he heard someone setting off a big firecracker down by the river.

As Mother Grey and Jack Kreevitch approached the Umbrella Works, search warrant in hand, they saw Ralph Voercker standing on the curb waiting to cross Bridge Street. "Ralph!" said Mother Grey. He started violently at the sound of his name.

"What are you doing here? Why aren't you at work?"

"I'm on the late shift tonight," he told her. "I was just walking. I wasn't doing anything."

"Good. Come with us, then," she said. "The church has been burglarized, and we have to go search for the loot."

"Burglarized?" he said. He seemed unusually agitated; she wondered whether he had remembered to take his meds that morning. In fact, he was acting so guilty that if she hadn't known better, Mother Grey would have suspected him of burglarizing the church himself. "What! They took things?"

"Somebody took our crucifix and my silver chalice and some other things."

"Who?"

"We don't know, but I think maybe Mr. Simon Ratcher knows something about it, so we're going to go and look around his place."

Ralph began raving. "There's no end to it, is there? Evil. It's everywhere. But we don't have to take it, Mother Vinnie. Even a Christian has ways."

She put what she hoped was a soothing hand on his arm. "Ralph, dear," she said, "did you remember to take your medication this morning?"

"I mean it, Mother Grey. Sometimes I think the Muslims have a better handle on certain things. We've been turning the other cheek long enough."

"What?"

"Cut off the head, and the body dies."

"What's with him?" murmured Kreevitch.

"He's upset about the burglary."

"He's not going to go crazy again, is he?"

"I'm sure he's fine," she said. "Come on, Ralph. We need your help." She took him firmly by the arm and led him to the front door of the Umbrella Works.

The store was not open. The sign on the door said CLOSED MONDAYS. Kreevitch knocked, banged, bellowed that he was a police officer, but nobody came to let them in. Somewhere in the depths of the building, they heard faint sounds, but it could have been rats or the wind.

Kreevitch looked at Mother Grey. "I suppose you expect me to break in," he said.

She said, "Why don't we try the back? I remember seeing doors to the sculpture garden." The path around the side had been shoveled. Still, it was made of flagstones, uneven in places and icy. They walked carefully. Ralph had to be pulled.

"I don't feel good, Mother Vinnie," said Ralph. "I want to go home now."

"Don't be silly," she told him. "Come on. We need you."

"Why?"

"Simon Ratcher keeps a million different objects in there. You can help Jack identify our things." They passed through the gap in the hedge. "He doesn't know what they look like."

Kreevitch said, "Let him go home, Mother Vinnie. He shouldn't be coming inside anyway. This is a police matter."

"Maybe you're right. We'll see you later then, Ralph." She patted his hand. But he didn't leave. He just stood there, looking nervous.

They were surprised to see the French doors standing wide open to the weather. "Let's go," said Kreevitch. "Wonder why he left 'em open. Police officer!" he shouted again.

Mother Grey followed Kreevitch into the drafty antiques store. "I hate to think what Ratcher's oil bill is going to be," she said. Out of the corner of her eye, she thought she saw Ralph scuffing his feet on the terrace and shifting the statues around.

"There it is, Jack!" St. Bede's processional crucifix was lying on top of a display case in plain view, quite near the doors. Belle-Mère's chalice was there, too, together with a number of other things that Mother Grey wouldn't have thought it worthwhile to steal, including her black vestments. Satanists! Pillaging her church! So where was the wretched Simon Ratcher?

Suddenly she saw protruding from behind the glass display case a pair of feet, toes down, encased in shoes with perfectly featureless soles, maybe a men's size nine. Or not. No, they were different from the shoes that had tramped mud all over her church, bigger, more rounded in the toes. But the important thing about them was, there were feet in them.

She put her hands to her head. "I don't want to do this anymore," she muttered.

"What?" said Kreevitch.

"Jack, I want you to look behind that case and tell me it isn't a body."

He looked, turned pale, and cursed.

"I guess it's a body, right?" she said. She took a look behind the case and at once regretted having done so. A half-second glance was more than enough.

"Come on out of here, Mother Vinnie. I'm gonna need some help on this one. Don't touch nothin'."

They went out the way they had come in. Ralph was still wiggling and jigging all over the terrace. Several of the statues seemed to have

134

been slightly rearranged. "Whatever in the world are you doing?" she said to him.

"Nothing," he said. "I mean, nothing." Kreevitch was using his police walkie-talkie, reporting the finding of a body, calling for help.

"A body?" said Ralph, suddenly very still.

"Yes, Ralph, I'm afraid we found a dead body in the Umbrella Works. It's almost certainly a case of foul play. Maybe you'd better run along now. Some other policemen will be here soon and—"

"It was me!" he began to yelp. "I did it! I did it! I did it all myself! Nobody else is involved!"

Kreevitch was very interested in Ralph's assertions. He clipped his radio back to his belt and got out his handcuffs. "Tell us about it," he said.

"I did it. It was me." Ralph was panting. "What do you want to know?"

"Maybe you can tell us first of all who it is."

"It's Rex Perskie. You can see that, you know him. Go look at his face."

"There ain't no face, son."

"What do you mean?"

"The head is gone. So tell us, Ralph. Before you cut this guy's head off, who was he?"

Ralph blinked. "Cut whose head off?"

"That's what I'm asking you."

"I didn't cut anybody's head off."

"That's not what you told us a minute ago."

Ralph frowned and shook his head as though to clear water from his ear. "His head? His head is off?" He sat down on a garden bench, heedless of the puddle of slush on the seat, and stared at the space between his feet. "I don't get it."

Mother Grey thought, *That bench isn't where it was when we got here. Ralph must have moved it. He must have moved all these things.* Kreevitch caught her eye and held it. She knew what he was thinking, and it had to do with summoning the men in white coats. *Do they still do that? Are there men in white coats?* Or with the trend toward de-institutionalization had the function of mental patient ambulances not been absorbed by other services, regular ambulance services, or police officers like Jack? Mother Grey had to confess that in all her thirty-seven years, she had never seen a white ambulance with mental attendants, outside of old movies. Someday someone would call for the men in white coats, and there wouldn't be any.

"I can tell you this," said Kreevitch. "It ain't Rex Perskie. Rex Perskie is a head shorter than this guy—or he used to be a head shorter—and his hands and arms were tattooed. There's no tattoos on this guy's arms. So who was it you wasted in there?"

Ralph was perfectly still for a long time. At last he said, "I guess I need to see a lawyer."

"Right," said Kreevitch. "You have a right to remain silent, you have a right to an attorney. . . . Hold your hands out, son, I need to put these cuffs on you."

"I'll call Martine," said Mother Grey.

"Call the paper-bag factory too, okay?" Ralph said. "Tell them I won't be in."

8

The temperature went up to 45 degrees Fahrenheit in Fishersville that afternoon. A few birds could be heard caroling the end of winter—prematurely, alas—and everything in town thawed and dripped.

On the Delaware, the ice was going out. Large irregularly shaped floes moved majestically southward, pointy ends first, flat white rafts carried on the breast of the swollen river under the bridge and away to the sea. Or at least to the wing dam. It was a tourist from New York who noticed that one of the rafts bore a passenger, lying very still, with his arm at an unnatural angle.

The tourist gazed at the still form for a minute or two, realized that it wasn't moving at all, and reported his observation to the bridge guard as she tried to keep warm in her little booth at the end of the bridge.

The bridge guard summoned the Fishersville Heavy Rescue Unit, the prize-winning local volunteers. It would take some doing to get the man off the ice before he went over the dam and into the hollow place underneath, the underwater cave from which few ever returned, and none alive.

A crowd began to gather. The heavy rescue team came with screaming sirens and launched their boat. Someone went for a videocamera.

Meanwhile Mother Grey and Martine Wellworth, Esq., huddled in the office in the undercroft of St. Bede's and tried to make a plan to save Ralph. They were conferring here rather than in Martine's office because the law firm she worked for was way off in Newark. Mother Grey did not want to travel to Newark, a journey of half an hour by car plus another hour by train, tedious even in the best of weather, although Martine, noble heroine of yuppiedom that she was, routinely made the trip three times a week.

Nevertheless Mother Grey was mortified at the appearance of her office. It needed paint; it smelled of the cigarettes Saraleigh persisted in smoking while she was practicing her typing; up above their heads the basement window, the only source of natural light, was dirty and full of leaves. In a couple of places there was even gum on the floor. The furniture—an old desk, two old chairs, and an old filing cabinet—was left over from Father Clentch, the priest who had been here before her. Most of the stationery had been his as well.

"It looks very bad, Mother Vinnie," said Martine.

"For Ralph, you mean," said Mother Grey. Of course, Martine would never make unpleasant remarks about her office, no matter how bad it looked.

"For Ralph, yes," she said.

Martine was trying to tell her something. A cold ugly feeling began at the base of Mother Grey's spine and traveled slowly upward. "Don't tell me you can't handle his case," she said.

"It's not as simple as that. You saw him." The two women had gone to see Ralph in the Fishersville police station right after he was arrested, while he waited for transportation to the jail in the county seat. The office smelled like paper and bad coffee, and a little bit like Ralph. They were holding him not in the sort of lockup Mother Grey had seen in the TV cop shows—a barred closet or whatever—but chained to a bench against the wall. Down under his knees was a bar parallel to the bench, and they had looped the handcuffs around it. The bench was big enough for three normal-sized prisoners. Ralph took up two places.

Even without the hunched posture enforced by being chained to a bar down around his ankles, poor Ralph would have been a study in dejection. He was hungry. He needed a bath. The police had taken his pills away. He kept scratching his nose on his shoulder.

"Don't ask me anything about what happened," he said. "I'll never tell. I'm going to take it to my grave."

"That's all right, Ralph," said Martine. "We'll talk later. I'm just here to see that your rights are protected."

"I don't want rights," he said. "Let them shoot me. Tell them to shoot me and get it over with. I have sinned."

It must have been then that Martine began to realize what they were up against. Her eyes met those of Mother Grey, and misgivings were written all over her face. Mother Grey patted her hand and reached out to pat Ralph's as well. The officer on duty said, "I'll have to ask you not to touch the prisoner, ma'am." He was a new man, slim, blond, his hair in a stiff brush cut. Nazis in the police station. Mother Grey pulled her hand back as if from a hot stove.

"Can we get you anything, dear?" she said to Ralph.

"Get them to execute me," he groaned. "Commend my soul to the Almighty." It was hard to remember the last time she had seen him so wretched. "Do they have a candy machine here?" he added.

Chief Harry seemed to have left his office door open; they could hear him guffawing into the phone. "Dental records? *Dental records?* Forget dental records, pal. There ain't no head."

Mother Grey asked the new Nazi policeman whether it would be all right if she gave the prisoner a candy bar. He said fine, then watched her closely while she put her two quarters into the machine. "A Twix bar, if they have it," Ralph called.

"They only have Snickers and Butterfingers."

"Butterfingers then," he said. As she unwrapped the candy bar, he said, "Put some cyanide in it. I don't want to live."

"Now, Ralph, calm down. It's going to be all right." She broke off pieces of the candy bar and put them in his mouth under the suspicious eye of the Nazi. As he swallowed the last one, Officer Jimmy Finn came in and said the van was here from the county.

"Up and at 'em, Ralph," Finn said, unlocking the cuff from his left wrist. "Time to go to the Blue Roof Hotel."

"Where's that?"

"County jail, my man," Finn said. He unlooped the chain from the bar and locked the cuff again.

"Oh. Okay. Good-bye, Mother Vinnie. Pray for me. Take care of Saraleigh and the kids after I'm gone."

"Take care of yourself, Ralph," she said. "Hang on and be brave. We're going to get you out of this."

"We'll talk later, Ralph," said Martine. "Don't answer any questions about the case unless I'm with you. I'll come see you in the jail." With Finn steering him by the elbow, he shuffled out.

141

Later Martine went to the county seat for the bail hearing. She got to speak with Ralph in private. He was still no help, taking the position that he would never talk, that he deserved whatever happened to him, that he only wanted to be left alone to suffer. The judge set bail at a million dollars, seeming to believe that Ralph was a dangerous lunatic best kept off the streets. Ralph himself didn't seem to care whether he stayed in jail or not. Even now he was under a suicide watch.

"It's so hard to find out what actually happened," said Martine, trying to explain the problem to Mother Grey. "Ralph won't cooperate, and I can't do a lot of legwork myself because I have to be in Newark on another case. Is there any money for a private investigator?"

"No," said Mother Grey.

At least Martine had been able to obtain a copy of the police report that Jack Kreevitch had made out. It bordered on incoherence, but that was the nature of the case. Although it was assumed that the body was that of Simon Ratcher, the proprietor of the antiques store, they didn't even know that for sure. The cause of death was also uncertain pending the autopsy; it was again assumed to be decapitation. A bloody hatchet had been found in the woodpile. No clear fingerprints. The report mentioned the burglary of St. Bede's and how the proceeds had been found near the body.

"So they picked on Ralph for a suspect right

away," said Martine. "How come? What does Ralph have to do with the Umbrella Works?"

"I guess he was standing around looking suspicious, Martine, and then as soon as the body was found, he began to shout, 'I did it! I killed him!' Basically, that was it."

"Might not be admissible," Martine murmured, making a note.

"It seemed to Jack that he was confessing."

"What I can't figure out was why he would confess. Unless he did it."

"He didn't actually confess."

"The report here quotes him saying, 'It was me, I did it, I did it, I killed him.' In so many words."

"I had the impression that he was talking about someone else. Or something he imagined. He seemed to think the body was Rex Perskie's."

"Saraleigh's old boyfriend? Is he still around?"

"He was seen in town on Saturday. Mrs. van Buskirk said he came to the apartment looking for Saraleigh while she was minding the children during the wedding shower. She told him, 'Go away, Saraleigh doesn't live here.' Evidently he didn't believe her, for on Sunday morning he came back, found Saraleigh at home, and attacked her."

"Oh, no. How is she?"

"She's pretty tough, I think she'll be okay. But Ralph was upset."

"Upset enough to go out and kill someone?"

"It seems so unlike him," said Mother Grey.

"Ordinarily, you see, people don't confess to

murders they haven't committed unless they're trying to shield somebody else, or unless they have deep feelings of guilt for some other reason and want to be punished for the other thing, so they confess to something they didn't do."

"I know Ralph is neurotic, but I don't really believe he's as sick as all that."

"He's definitely disturbed, Vinnie. I'm seriously thinking that his best bet might be a plea of insanity. You know he's been in and out of mental institutions for years."

"He couldn't have murdered Simon Ratcher."

"Maybe he has an alibi. What was he doing while the real killer was murdering Simon Ratcher?"

"I don't know."

"Then the first thing we have to do is find out. I'm going to have a hard time defending him without knowing what actually happened."

"He didn't kill Simon Ratcher."

"Yes, you keep saying that, but let me ask you this. What makes you think he didn't?"

"I know him. He could never do such a thing."

"Why not?"

"Ralph Voercker doesn't have a violent bone in his body."

" 'The neighbors said he was such a quiet boy.' "

"No, really, Martine. You know Ralph. He's not a violent person. Unless he's provoked."

"For instance, if he catches somebody robbing

his church. I know how he cares for the church, Mother Vinnie."

"Yes, or . . . no. Really. Not Ralph."

"Or if someone beats up his girlfriend."

Mother Grey was silent.

"Has anyone seen Rex Perskie recently?" Martine asked. "Or maybe Saraleigh did something to Rex, and she's the one Ralph is trying to shield."

"Jack thinks Rex left town yesterday."

"But he isn't sure, right? We should try to find him. Did Ralph ever mention to you what he was doing at the Umbrella Works in the first place?"

"No."

"Okay, then, since we can't hire an investigator, we'll have to do it ourselves. Here's what I need you to do, Mother Vinnie. Find out for me what he was doing that he doesn't want to talk about."

"All right. I'll try."

"See if Saraleigh knows, or his friends at the halfway house. Meanwhile I'll try to get his bail reduced."

"I hope you can. I'd feel more comfortable if he were out of jail," said Mother Grey.

"All we really have to do when the case comes to trial is to establish a reasonable doubt," said Martine. "But if we aren't able do that, he'll surely have no trouble pleading insanity."

"I'd sooner clear his name entirely. Ralph is having a hard enough time achieving success in life without being followed around by a reputation as a homicidal maniac."

"Of course," said Martine. "Naturally." But did she mean it? Was she passionately committed to clearing Ralph's name? Mother Grey suspected not. Of course, naturally, she would do it if she could. But what Ralph needed right now was an advocate totally devoted to his interests, neck or nothing. Saraleigh fit that description, but she had no skill in matters of confrontation with the law. Mother Grey fit the description also—almost— but there was something else she was supposed to do this week, if only she could remember—

Martine got up, stuffing her notes into her briefcase. "I have to go. The baby-sitter has a fit if I don't pick up Henry before her husband gets home. By the way, Mother Vinnie, isn't St. Bede's day-care center supposed to open soon?"

A cold hand clutched at Mother Grey's heart. "Two weeks from today," she said, "provided we pass inspection tomorrow. It's good you reminded me. This business with Ralph has driven everything else out of my mind."

"A lot of us are counting on it," said Martine. "The woman who watches Henry has too many kids there. Last Friday I almost stepped on a little baby she left just layin' on the floor."

"My word."

"There was one poor little boy vomiting in the kitchen, crying for his mother."

"I'm surprised you leave Henry there."

"Have to leave him somewhere. Can't take him to the office, and Al and I can't swing a nanny just yet." Martine put on her coat. "Now remember what I told you. It's going to take a lot of work to get to the bottom of this, and I have to spend the next three days in Newark on another case."

"We need a plan," said Mother Grey.

"We need to find out what the story is," said Martine. "We need to find out what happened to the head."

After Martine left, Mother Grey sat for a long time at her desk in the office of St. Bede's making lists, trying to unravel this crazy tangle by the application of logic.

Start with the questions.

Whose is the body? Is it really Simon Ratcher's?

She thought back to the instant when she had seen the headless corpse on the floor of the store. It had been no more than an instant, for she hadn't wanted to see it and looked away at once, but that instant left a snapshot in her mind. The corpse lay on its . . . face? Let's say it lay on its belly, at an angle to the display case, with its arms down at its sides. Quite a peaceful posture, really. The translucent shadow of the oak and glass case fell across the upper part of the torso. The left foot and part of the left leg rested on a small burgundy-and-black oriental rug, a lovely little rug; the rest of the body was lying right on the cold concrete floor in a little puddle of . . . in a little puddle that didn't stain the rug, it was good that the rug had been spared. The body was dressed all in black, baggy pants and a turtleneck sweater. For the rest of her life, Mother Grey would have trouble with turtleneck sweaters. These certainly appeared to be Simon Ratcher's clothes. Of course it was Simon Ratcher. But actually it could have been anybody about Simon's size, even a woman, from all Mother Grey had seen. She shut off the picture in her mind, or tried to, and wrote down the next question:

Where is the head?
Why decapitation?
Who did it?
What was Ralph doing while all this was going on?

She wrote the questions down on a legal pad, but they seemed pointless and empty. She was not inspired. She even tried to visualize the dirty deed itself, but it was so hard to see the sophisticated Simon Ratcher offering his neck to a person with a hatchet. There was something wrong with the picture. Maybe these weren't the right questions.

She called the halfway house for disturbed young men, just to see how Schwartz was coming with his investigations into Satanism. The line was busy. Schwartz must be off on another cruise of the information superhighway.

Then she thought, *Ash Wednesday*. Now that Ralph was locked up in the Blue Roof Hotel, she would need to line up another acolyte for mass, and that meant Edward Warthen.

She called the Warthen house. Their phone was busy too. It seemed like a good time for a walk, so she bundled up, put Towser on his lead, and walked the few blocks to the old Wagonner mansion, where the Warthens were living.

9

Before she went up the steps to knock at the door, Mother Grey paused in the driveway to admire the Wagonner mansion's garage, or carriage house as it must once have been called. The structure had two floors, all the fanciest Victorian gingerbread, and a cupola. The last rays of sunset caught the copper weathervane. It was shaped like an umbrella, a reminder of the foundation of the Wagonner family fortunes. Ellen was lucky to have such a place for her studio, if it wasn't too drafty. Many a local artist would kill for a space like that to work in. Mother Grey wondered whether the local historical preservation buffs or the zoning officer would give them a hard time if they tried to put skylights in. Skylights weren't all that Victorian. Of course, it depended on how you did them.

No lights were on in the carriage house, but Mother Grey and her dog went up and peeked in the garage-door windows to see whether Ellen Warthen might be inside working. It would be good to have a private talk with Ellen, maybe find out whether she had any concerns about Edward and Satanism—Edward and unhealthy pursuits—

The inside of the garage was quite dark, but in the little light that filtered through the windows, Mother Grey could see that it was not yet ready to be used as a painting studio. The concrete floor had been largely cleared off, as though preparations were under way, but things, very large things in some cases, were piled up against the south wall in such haphazard fashion that surely even to look at this disorder would quell anyone's desire to make art. Lawn mowers, playhouses, garden furniture were all jumbled together.

Perhaps the Warthens were planning a garage sale. In any case, it appeared that they were staging this stuff for relocation elsewhere. The very idea of the heiress to the Sedgewick fortune holding a garage sale caused Mother Grey to laugh, at which sound Towser sat down in the snow and raised one bushy eyebrow at her. As soon as his bottom was cold, he got up again. She took him up on the front step and employed the brass knocker.

It was not Ellen who came to answer the door

but the major. Aha! Alcohol on his breath. But was he merely indulging in the genteel custom of a snort before dinner, or was he on a bender? "I didn't want to disturb you," she said, "but the phone was busy, and I wanted to ask Edward to serve Wednesday night."

"I'm glad to see you, Mother Vinnie," he said. "Come in." The major's smile was something she rarely saw. It had a forlorn quality to it. She looped Towser's lead around the porch railing, scratched the dog behind the ear, and went into the Warthens' warm house.

A number of Ellen's paintings hung in the hall, expensively framed. She was very good at what she did.

"Edward!" the major called up the stairs.

"Yeah, what?" a small voice called back.

"Yes, sir!" the major corrected.

Edward appeared at the top of the stairs. "Yes, sir?"

"Are you two still tying up the phone?"

"No, sir."

"Mother Grey came to see you. She has something to ask you. Come down."

"Yes, sir." He came pounding down the stairs, followed by the same pale dark-haired boy she had seen at Celia's wedding. Since the light was better here than in the Umbrella Works, she could see now that the other boy's hair was shaved all the way up the back and over his ears. He wore a denim jacket, open to reveal part of a gray T-shirt with pictures and writing on it. All that Mother

Grey could see of the shirt was a single bloodshot eye and some random lettering. It was probably just as well. She hated rude sayings on clothing.

"Hi, Mother Vinnie."

"Hello, Edward. I came to ask whether you could serve Wednesday night," said Mother Grey. "Ralph is—ah—incapacitated."

His eyes went to the other boy. "Wednesday night?" he said.

The other boy murmured, "Wednesday night. Sure."

"Sure," Edward said. "What time?"

"Seven-thirty."

"See you then. We're going bowling, Dad," Edward said, getting a winter jacket out of the closet. The dark-haired boy carried a bowling bag.

"There's an alley in Fishersville?"

"Frenchtown. Adam's mom is driving us." The two rushed out the front door, slamming it behind themselves.

" 'Yeah, what,' " the major grumbled. "This is what comes of spending time with town kids. 'Yeah, what.' Tell me something, Mother Vinnie. What do you know about that kid Adam?"

"Nothing at all. Is his name Adam?"

"I thought you knew everyone in town."

"No, I can't say I do."

"I don't know half these kids Edward keeps company with. They come over here and close themselves in his room and do God knows what on his computer. I think they dial out somehow. Our phone bill is astronomical."

152

"It could be worse," said Mother Grey. "Computers are supposed to be educational at least."

"Worse," he said. He was silent for a long time, his brows knitted. Something was on his mind. Then he said, "Ellen doesn't supervise Edward properly. Some of these people should never have been allowed near him. This Adam is one of them."

"Is Ellen around? I really wanted to talk to her."

"No, she's not here."

"When do you think she'll be back?"

He pushed his glasses up and stood rubbing his eyes for a good minute. "I guess there's no point in keeping it from you any longer," he said at last. "Ellen has left us."

Mother Grey was shocked. Whatever she had expected to hear, this was not it. "I'm so sorry."

"I can't even say for certain where she's gone. She's done this to us before; usually she stays at a hotel in the city. But this time I have a feeling she isn't coming back."

"The city?"

"Manhattan, the Hotel Inter-continental. I called last night to see if she was there. The clerk said she wasn't registered, but I think she might be staying under an assumed name. Would you like a drink?"

"No, thank you," she said. It was true that the sun was over the yardarm, but Mother Grey usually confined her tippling to an after-dinner sherry or two. "I'd better get Towser home." The major poured himself a brandy; his hand trembled slightly. Mother Grey concluded that he was upset and suspected that he was indeed on a bender.

He grimaced when he put the drink to his lips. "What the hell—?"

"Something wrong?"

"This isn't brandy. Tastes like maple syrup and water. What's the big idea of this? Ellen, I suppose, trying to cure me of my so-called alcoholism. I don't know who she thought it would fool."

Mother Grey took the bottle with the Courvoisier label and smelled it, as much to verify the soundness of the major's mind and perceptions as to commiserate with him. Sure enough, there was no alcohol in that bottle.

"Maybe the boys—?" she said.

"Adam," said the major. "That little bastard. Now he's stealing my liquor."

10

It was dark out by the time Mother Grey got back to her office, there to clear up a few things before braving the confusion and noise of a rectory occupied by Saraleigh Kane and her children. Actually she was putting off going home until she was fairly certain that all of the children were asleep and Saraleigh was tucked up somewhere with a ladies' magazine. Dinner would be a reprise of yesterday's, Saraleigh's beef stew reheated in the microwave. She was looking forward to putting her feet up on the ottoman and eating it all by herself with the glow of the fire in her face.

Granny would never have approved of Vinnie's having supper in the living room, still less in her stocking feet. But that was then. Mother Grey could no longer keep it up: dinner in the dining room every night, candles on the table, linen napkins. The old correct ways, the ways of elegance, had probably died with her grandmother. Look at Dave Dogg, the way he held his fork. *Could I ever have taught the children of such a man to eat properly?* It was something to think about.

She heard sounds at the office door, and then a knock. The major's runaway wife! But, no, it was only Marla Kreevitch carrying and dragging her three smallest children. "Come in, Marla," said Mother Grey.

"I'm sorry to disturb you," said Marla.

"It's quite all right."

"I wanted to talk to you about the day-care center. Martine told me there were papers to fill out, so I came over. Jack is on duty tonight. I had to bring the little guys."

The little guys were Bobby, two and a half, Jennifer, four, and Elizabeth, five. "Where are Brian and Christopher?" said Mother Grey.

"Cub Scouts. Here's the thing, Vinnie. I got a call from an old friend at the medical center. They're hiring nurses right now, but it might not be for long. If I don't jump on this, it won't be there for me later."

"I thought nurses had an easy time finding jobs."

"Not in this part of the country. If we wanted to relocate, I wouldn't have any problem, but things are tight here right now. I know graduates from nursing school who can't find a thing."

DEVIL'S WORKSHOP

"Is this going to be a full-time job?"

"No, it's part-time, that's what makes it ideal. Only three days a week, and only during school hours. It would be a great thing if I could take it," she said. "The city isn't raising salaries for the police this year. But as I said, I talked to Martine about it, and she filled me in about the problems. I really don't want to leave Bobby and Jennifer with her sitter."

"I think Martine's sitter has more than enough children to take care of, from what Martine says," Mother Grey said. "How soon would your job begin?"

"A week from next Monday. That's when the day-care center will open, isn't it? Martine said so."

"That's what we're shooting for," said Mother Grey. It was coming up uncomfortably fast. "The inspection is tomorrow. Hopefully they won't find any deficiencies serious enough to keep us from opening."

She took out the black-and-white composition book where she kept the enrollment records for the yet-to-be-opened child-care center. Among those on the waiting list were Martine's boy Henry and Saraleigh's baby girls. From time to time Saraleigh made noises about looking for a job, saying she would take one if only she could find a place to park the kids. Mother Grey wrote the names of Robert and Jennifer Kreevitch at the bottom. That made twenty children for the center.

"Here are the papers you need to fill out," said

Mother Grey. "You can bring them back here any-time in the next few days."

"Thanks," said Marla. "I'll do that."

"Good luck with the job."

"Good luck with the day-care center." She hefted Bobby, who was beginning to whimper, over her shoulder and gathered up her purse.

Again there was a knock at the office door. Mother Grey sprang up and opened it, and there stood Deacon Deedee Gilchrist, holding out a worn red book, slightly larger than a prayer book: *The Book of Ceremonial Magic* by Arthur Edward Waite.

"Canon Spelving said you could borrow this. It has all the *Grimorium Verum* spells in English. You won't have to translate. I was going to FedEx it, but they said they were having delays with their schedules because of the weather, so I . . . I'm sorry. I'm interrupting."

"Hi, Deedee," said Marla. "It's okay, come in. I was just putting the kids on the list for the child-care center."

"St. Bede's Child Care Center!" said Deedee. "I had forgotten all about it. Gracious. When is it due to open?"

"We hope the center will be opening a week from next Monday," Mother Grey said. "But it de-pends on how the state inspection goes tomor-row."

"I'll pray for you," said Marla.

"Good. We need all the help we can get."

"I think it's wonderful that you're doing this.

We all do. You were the last person we would have thought would start a day-care center."

"I was? Why?"

"Well, you know, you're so . . . It's just wonderful that you're doing it, is all. Have a nice night. Come on, Jenny."

Marla went out, pulling four-year-old Jennifer by the hand. Little Bobby took his thumb out of his mouth, sighed, and gave them a very serious brown-eyed look over his mother's shoulder.

"Whatever did she mean?" said Mother Grey, as soon as all the Kreevitches were out of earshot.

"She meant, dear, that you seem uncomfortable around small children. I can't believe that you're unaware of it."

"*Moi?*"

"But not to worry, you're hiring competent staff for this enterprise. You've selected four or five of the best candidates from this pile of résumés here on your desk and scheduled interviews with them. Yes?"

Mother Grey began to pull her hair. "I haven't got to them," she moaned.

"Something wrong?" said Deedee. "Aside from the day-care center inspection?"

"Ralph has been arrested for murder."

"Good heavens. Does he have a lawyer?"

"Martine is defending him, but there are problems."

"Who was murdered?"

"That's one of the problems. They think it's this antique dealer, but whoever killed him cut his head off, so there's been some trouble making a positive identification."

"Good heavens," she said again.

"Since you went home yesterday morning, we've had an attempted rape, a burglary at the church, and now a murder," said Mother Grey. "And I think Dave is going to dump me and return to his ex-wife. Somehow in the confusion I completely forgot about the rising tide of Satanism. But thanks for the book."

"You're welcome. Good heavens. Murder? And what's this about Dave?"

"I don't know. He called me from Boston. I really don't know what's going on with him."

She took the book in her hands and riffled through it.

"You've been neglecting him, maybe," said Deedee.

"Maybe." There were a lot of line drawings in the book, strange symbols that reminded her of Celtic knots. Confusing. "I'm not sure I can deal with this right now," she said.

"The book? Or Dave?"

"Either one. Somehow I don't think Satanist spells have anything to do with my troubles at this point."

"You never know," Deedee said. "They don't call him the Evil One for nothing."

"Martine says what we really need is a detective."

"No doubt," said Deedee.

"I don't mean a Trenton homicide detective, I

mean a private detective we could hire. If we had any money."

Deedee said, "So what about these day-care inspectors?"

"Coming tomorrow." Mother Grey found herself actually wringing her hands.

"I take it the day-care center hasn't been at the top of your to-do list this week."

"Saraleigh and the kids are in the rectory again. That, if you remember, was where the day-care center was supposed to be."

"Oops."

They both knew what that meant: finger marks, cigarette butts, diapers, chaos, and filth. When Saraleigh and her children inhabited a space, it soon lost all fitness for habitation by children, certainly according to the standards of state inspectors. "Maybe I can get her to help me straighten up," said Mother Grey. "If she understands how important it is. They're coming to inspect at nine in the morning."

"I'll help. Let's go."

They locked up the church and rushed next door to the rectory. Saraleigh was not there. A note on the kitchen table explained that she had been to see Ralph in the county jail, and she now felt that it was safe to take the children and move back into her apartment. *Rex won't be bothering us*, she said. *Thanks for everything. P.S. Do you think you can get Ralphie out?*

" 'Rex won't be bothering us.' Why does this

not come as music to my ears?" Mother Grey said. Her bad feeling was growing worse, if possible.

"Poor girl," said Deedee. "They were supposed to have been married on Saturday."

"Maybe we can still get him out in time for the wedding," said Mother Grey. "If we can clear him somehow."

"How?"

"Don't know."

"You need a bold plan, Vinnie."

"I guess the thing to do is solve the murder."

"First let's clean up the rectory."

By midnight, Deedee and Mother Grey had finished cleaning. The last cache of smelly cigarette butts had been removed from under a radiator and discarded, the last disposable diaper disposed of, the last wad of gum pried from the hardwood floor. Old Horace Burkhardt's ancestral home, which he had sold to the church when the old rectory burned down, was spotless again, ready to shelter and nurture the twenty or so small children that Mother Grey was expecting on opening day. Mother Grey and Deedee were exhausted.

"Let's have tea," said Deedee, and put the kettle on. While Deedee collected the cups and waited for the water to boil, Mother Grey flipped absently through Arthur Spelving's copy of *Ceremonial Magic*. There seemed to be several chapters on preparing tools, how to make parchment suitable for writing spells, how to make pens and ink. What an extraordinary reverence these ancients had for the act of reading and writing, a commonplace activity in our time. Then there was a chapter on the drawing of various symbols to call demonic spirits, and at last the particular spells to work your will on a grudging universe.

While Mother Grey looked through the spells, Deedee felt impelled to read the sayings on the supermarket tea bags. " 'Shepherds never have the wool pulled over their eyes.' Why do you suppose they put this stuff on tea bags?"

"I don't know, Deedee. Some old custom of telling fortunes with tea."

"These aren't even fortunes. They're nothing but moronic non sequiturs."

"I never read them. The tea is cheap and good."

"I can't imagine who writes these. Certainly not the same person who does those pithy fortunes in Chinese cookies. Wait, here's a good one. I'll put it in my cup. It says 'Fortune favors the bold.' Perfectly sensible."

The spell Mother Grey was reading so consumed her attention that she became aware only gradually that Deedee was chattering at her. *"Begin this operation on a Wednesday before the sun rises, being furnished with seven black beans. Take next the severed . . ."* "What did you say, Deedee?"

" 'Fortune favors the bold.' It's a sign, Vinnie."

"What sort of sign?"

"It's a sign that you and I need to break into Simon Ratcher's apartment and search it." Appropriately, the cuckoo clock peeped twelve.

"You're talking about committing a felony," said Mother Grey.

"Only if we get caught." Deedee licked the honey off her teaspoon.

Mother Grey put aside the book of black magic. "You feel that this will improve the situation?"

"Vinnie, you're obviously very unhappy. You feel that Martine is too conservative in her approach to Ralph's case, and you'll never forgive yourself if you don't do everything you can to exonerate him. Am I right?"

"Yes, you're right."

"I hate to see you in misery. Seize the moment."

Suddenly Mother Grey felt a lifting sensation as though an unseen foot had been removed from her neck. Her friend was indeed right. Where better to begin saving Ralph than by examining the living quarters of his supposed victim? What better time than midnight? But for breaking and entering, they would need rum in the tea. The bottle left over from the Christmas punch was under the sink. She drew it forth and sloshed it into the tea mugs. "I believe he lived right near Delio's. He used to get breakfast there. We can find his address in the telephone book. But tell me, Deedee, what is it we're looking for?"

"Clues," said Deedee, peering at her over the top of her bifocals through the steam of the tea. "Presumably we'll know them when we see them."

"Martine isn't going to like this."

DEVIL'S WORKSHOP

"Martine doesn't have to hear about it."

"Unless we have to call her from the police station. And Rupert Bingley. What do you think he would say? 'Mother Grey, you're finished in Fishersville.'"

"Hush."

She downed the rum-filled tea and was assaulted suddenly by other misgivings. "Deedee, I want you to understand something."

"Yes, dear."

"We aren't doing this to make me feel better."

"Oh, no, no."

"This is for the furtherance of justice."

"Justice. Yes."

"Let's go."

They dressed in long underwear and pale sweatsuits so as to blend in with the snowy night. When they went out, they found that the town had frozen up again after sunset. Footing was bad. The householders of Fishersville had dug trenches in the snow where the sidewalks went, one snow shovel wide, between their property lines, as a gesture toward clearing the way. In the daytime the melting snow collected at the bottom of these trenches, and at night it froze slick and glassy. The snow on either side of each trench had a crust over it that was treacherous and noisy to step on.

Deedee slipped and nearly fell for the third time. "Walk in the street," said Mother Grey. They walked in the street, bathed in bright moonlight, and then they jogged a little where the cars had cleared enough of a path, because they were cold

165

and because Deedee wanted to work off her cholesterol. Four blocks away was Bridge Street, the heart of the central business district, two- and three-story single-family residences and apartments mixed in with storefronts. The city Christmas lights were still up on every lamppost; they glimmered red and green on the heaped snow underneath.

No one was out. It was so quiet that you could hear the traffic light change from yellow to red, *bzzt-poink*. The two women could see their own breath hanging out in front of them.

They crossed against the red light, throwing law and order to the winds. Ratcher lived on the second floor over the collectible toy store. There was a door that must have opened onto his stairway, but it was locked. "Let's try the back," said Deedee. "There must be a fire escape or some such thing."

The row of houses and stores presented an impenetrable front until they came to a house several doors down that had a side alley leading to a garden in the back. Cold winds blew through the alley; sand and salt crunched softly underfoot. Reaching the back, they saw that gaining what they presumed to be the fire escape to Ratcher's apartment was a simple matter of wriggling through a number of hedges and vaulting a fence. Duck soup.

On they pressed. Behind them their footprints showed plainly in the snow, and before them dogs were stirring in their apartments, woofing softly almost as though in their sleep. The rum was wearing off. Mother Grey began to think that what she was doing was probably stupid. She tore her jacket on the second hedge. She tore her pants on the third. As they crept toward the fire escape that led to Ratcher's second-floor apartment, the crust on the snow began to make hideously loud crunching noises whenever they put their feet down.

It seemed to the women then that their progress could be plainly heard by everyone in Fishersville. At last they reached the foot of the ladder that led to the fire escape, only to find it coated with a thick integument of ice. In the shadows here nothing would melt until spring.

Slowly and at great peril they climbed up to the platform outside what must have been Ratcher's bathroom window, frosted all over as it was with curlicue patterns that kept them from seeing in. Mother Grey pushed on it a little with gloved hands. It stuck, painted shut probably, then gave about an inch. Not locked.

A dog in the third-floor apartment began to bark. Someone up there was moving around, then pushing up the window corresponding to the one in front of which they now crouched.

Under cover of the sound of the other window opening, which made a shuddering great racket, Mother Grey pushed Ratcher's bathroom window all the way up and wriggled through the opening. Deedee followed. For an awful moment they feared she might get stuck. Someone upstairs was shouting: "Hey! Who's out there!"

The huge white-tiled bathroom in which they found themselves smelled of sandalwood and patchouli. Towels were neatly piled on a chrome stand. There was a big walk-in shower. Deedee played her penlight over it and revealed multiple shower heads. "Very nice," she said. "I bet he has a Jacuzzi and a bidet." Further exploration with the penlight revealed that this was indeed the case.

"This is madness," said Mother Grey. "The neighbor upstairs is calling the police right now."

"We'd better be quick, then."

"What are we looking for?"

"Evidence of Satanist connections, names and phone numbers of Ratcher's associates, women's clothing, wolf's clothing, sheep's clothing, anything." Trusting that Deedee's familiarity with westerns had equipped her with the correct mindset for adventures of this nature, Mother Grey followed her out into the main room of Simon Ratcher's apartment.

Ratcher had lived surrounded by chrome and white leather, consistent with the starkest sort of New York City artistic taste. The clutter that characterized his place of business was totally absent from his home. By the light of Deedee's penlight, they saw that the apartment seemed to consist of the bathroom, a tiny kitchen like a sailboat's galley, and one big room for living and sleeping, extending all the way to the front of the house.

On the floor of the kitchen Deedee's penlight revealed a young black cat, hardly out of kittenhood. It cried in rather a sweet voice and looked hungry. She picked it up.

"Here's his desk," Mother Grey said. There were business papers on it, including a bill for more than three hundred dollars' worth of photographic supplies.

"So Simon Ratcher was a photographer along with everything else," said Mother Grey. "Maybe that's a clue."

"Or it could be that he took pictures of his wares for out-of-town customers," said Deedee. The top drawer held a tin cookie box. Inside was a plastic bag full of some herbal substance and a number of twisted-up cigarettes. "Joints," Deedee marveled.

"Indeed?" said Mother Grey.

The cat purred loudly against Deedee's chest. She stroked its head. "Poor little fellow, nobody left to feed you."

In the shadows they suddenly saw someone else moving around in the room with a tiny light: two burglars, one plump, one slim, in sweatsuits, watch caps, and big floppy gloves. Deedee gasped. "It's us," said Mother Grey. A mirrored wall concealed a long closet redolent of sandalwood, and yes, there were women's clothes in there, a couple of feathered negligees hanging from blue satin padded hangers. Did this mean Ratcher entertained women? Who knew? Maybe he wore them

169

himself. Mother Grey thought she heard a sound on the fire escape. "Let's get out of here."

"Wait a minute—aha." Ratcher's personal telephone directory lay on a glass and chrome table beside the bed. Deedee grabbed it and stuck it in her pocket.

At the bathroom window where they had come in, there was a rattling, and again a voice called, "Hey! You in there!"

Frantically Deedee played the penlight around the white walls, looking for the front way out. Another voice came from the window. "Go back inside your apartment, please, sir. We'll handle it now." Good heavens, it was Jack Kreevitch. He was coming in the back. Next to the kitchen there was another door; the women opened it, rushed through, and found themselves in a stairwell. Down they went, making no noise whatever until Mother Grey stepped on a big manila envelope lying at the foot of the stairs on a soft rug. It caused her foot to slip, and she let out a little yip.

"What's that?" whispered Deedee, training her penlight on it.

The front door was right there, and the mail slot. "It's Simon's mail," Mother Grey said, looking down at the envelope. There was something odd about the address. "Look at this. It's addressed to Simon Ratcher, but the return address is the Umbrella Works. He mailed it to himself."

They could hear Jack's voice through the closed door at the top of the stairs: "Police officers! Come out and show yourself!"

"Get that envelope," whispered Deedee, who was herself busy clutching the cat. Mother Grey was now so steeped in depravity that robbing the U.S. mails was as nothing to her. She scooped up the manila envelope, thick with cardboard, and stuffed it under her jacket. With only the faintest of clicks, Deedee opened the street door.

The Nazi had stationed himself by the narrow alley that led around to the back. By the grace of God, his face was turned away from them as they tiptoed out onto the sidewalk.

"Let's run," Deedee whispered.

"Let's run toward him," Mother Grey whispered back. "Make believe we're joggers. Come on." They closed the door noiselessly. Then with exaggerated puffing and blowing noises, they huffed past the policeman, and so accustomed was he to lady joggers that he barely glanced at them. It's the unusual that attracts a policeman's attention. Presumably the Nazi did not consider it unusual for a plump, gray-haired midnight jogger to be clutching a small black cat to her breast.

Around the corner and halfway up the block, they slowed down and began to stroll, affecting an appearance of nonchalance. Mother Grey's heart was pounding. Her friend's forehead was bedewed with sweat, even in the freezing cold.

"That was invigorating," said Deedee. "But I did rather think I was going to have a heart attack."

"I thought you were too," said Mother Grey. "Now what?"

"We'll get this address book and Ratcher's envelope back to the rectory and take a good look."

"Wait a minute. What if one of these contains some sort of important clue?" said Mother Grey. "The chain of evidence is broken. It won't stand up in a court of law."

"You've been watching those police docudramas again."

"Yes, I have. I keep thinking it will give me some understanding of what Dave is all about."

"Why don't you just marry him?"

Marry him? "If I did that, the understanding would come too late." *Marry him.* "Do you really think I should marry him, Deedee?" *But what if he doesn't come back?*

"I think you should have married him the first time he asked you. I also think you should buy another cello. But no cello can ever be as good as the Weaver, and no man can ever compare with Stephen. So here you are, tending your shrines when you could be making beautiful music."

"Maybe you're right," said Mother Grey. "But I'm not sure the offer is still open." Was it really time to think of marrying again? Next month Stephen Grey would be dead ten years. She no longer thought of him any more often than two or three times a day. *My first husband.* How did that sound?

"As for the address book and the envelope," Deedee said, "if we find anything in them, we'll simply break into Ratcher's apartment again and put them back."

11

—————————————————————————

S now came hissing down out of the gray sky of morning as Mother Grey, dead for sleep, nailed her new sign to the front door of the rectory: ST. BEDE'S COMMUNITY CHILD CARE CENTER. When the child-care facility inspection team from the State of New Jersey came for their preliminary inspection, they would at least be able to find the place.

The rectory that Mother Grey was attempting to convert into a day-care center was not very big, although as a residence it was spacious by Fishersville standards. Built of brick, easily a hundred years old, the house was laid out like a row house, although you could walk around it: two stories and an attic, three rooms on each story. The backyard at least was sizable, thirty by fifty feet, and fenced, good for a play yard. After the old rectory burned, the diocese had allowed St. Bede's to use the insurance money to buy this place from Horace Burkhardt, now living next door in another one of his houses. Small as it was, it was still too big for a single woman priest with few possessions; it would be a waste of church resources to do nothing else with it but live there. And there was, so to speak, a crying need for day care. But Mother Grey wasn't at all certain that it was up to code according to state regulations, or that it could be in two weeks, irrespective of her personal qualifications to run a day-care center.

Canon Arthur Spelving of Holy Assumption in Ocean Prospect, Mother Grey's mentor in matters of interaction with state government, had sent her a photocopy of the state laws regarding day-care facilities, 176 pages long. With the imminent arrival of the inspectors, she began to feel that she had not studied it enough. She had, perhaps, fallen asleep in the middle of important chapters. (Mother Grey did much of her studying in bed.) Furthermore it contained frequent references to the state building code and the state fire code, of which she did not have copies. Unprepared. Anxiety like this had not plagued her since her days in Virginia Theological Seminary. It was that old feeling: Today is the exam. And there was something else.

It seemed to Mother Grey that Simon Ratcher's pornographic pictures of young boys were emitting waves like radiation, streams of evil energy that could not help but be detected by the inspectors when they came. Normally there would be no reason for anyone to go into her office in the basement of St. Bede's, no reason for anyone to open the bottom drawer and look inside any manila envelopes they might find there. But the horrible envelope was throbbing on the ether, like Poe's telltale heart. How could they overlook it?

Naturally she and Deedee had steamed the envelope open as soon as they got back to the rectory. None of this "We'll sleep on this evidence and then look at it tomorrow," while murderers and culprits of every stripe crept in and stole it away unexamined, or burned the house down around their ears and the envelope with it. Gingerly Mother Grey had worked the photographs, encased between cardboard, out of their envelope, careful to leave no fingerprints; eagerly she had inspected them; instantly she was sorry. But she couldn't un-look at them, any more than she could expunge from her mind the image of the headless corpse, lying in shadow with its foot on the red and black rug.

Deedee had insisted on seeing what was in the envelope to make her turn so pale. When Mother Grey handed her the pictures, holding them carefully by the edges to keep them free of fingerprints, Deedee took one look and dropped them right into her tea. Then Mother Grey began to weep, not because they had been caught like Bluebeard's wife with a spot of blood on the fatal key, not even because she was dead tired, but because innocence betrayed and perverted is a very sad thing.

Deedee cleaned up the pictures until only a slight brown stain was left. When they were dry, she put them back in the manila envelope. "Surely these are evidence," said Mother Grey. She thought she recognized one of the boys, a shiftless youth given to idling about town on a skateboard. "They might have something to do with the murder."

"Put them back through the mail slot as soon as it gets dark again," Deedee said. "Nobody has to know we ever had them. The police will just think they're something they overlooked." So she put them in her drawer in the office.

Perhaps the inspectors would be held up by the storm. The weather was terrible; yet another travel advisory had been issued; perhaps they wouldn't come at all. She went inside and called the state to find out whether the child-care facility inspection team was going to be traveling to Fishersville in spite of the weather, and they said yes, expect them at nine o'clock as arranged.

Mother Grey told herself she didn't really need a day's reprieve from the inspection. The rectory might be small, but it was surely adequate for fifteen or twenty young children. It was clean, bright, and cheerful and had a kitchen and two bathrooms—what could they find lacking? She picked up the ring binder of rules and flopped it open at random:

"... for existing buildings whose construction

code use group classification would change from that which it had been . . . the center shall obtain a Certificate of Occupancy (CO) issued by the municipality in which it is located, reflecting the center's compliance with the provisions of the NJUCC. . . ."

Well, how about it? Was the construction of the place up to the state code? She had meant to call the city inspector, but somehow time had passed and the call had never been made. Tomorrow. She would call him tomorrow. Or this afternoon. With luck there would be no really expensive violations, and they could have the place all shipshape by a week from Monday.

". . . ii. B (Business) for buildings accommodating children 2 1/2 years of age and/or older and having a total occupancy of more than five and fewer than fifty children . . . Certificate of Life/Safety Approval . . . New Jersey Uniform Fire Code . . . State Sanitary Code . . .

"If a child defecates in the swimming pool, all solid wastes shall be removed. . . ." There was no swimming pool here, so at least she wouldn't have to deal with that. She wondered what had caused the lawmakers in their wisdom to think of such an eventuality. Had they covered everything? Every single thing? Was there a clause in here prescribing what to do if the sponsor defecated in fear at the approach of the state inspectors?

At that moment a car bearing the state seal on its door pulled up to the curb, and the state inspectors got out.

The inspectors were dressed to kill: the man wore a raincoat, dark suit, and ominously quiet tie, and the two women were attired with similarly menacing formality in business suits, hose, and high heels. No white gloves, at least. Mother Grey went out to face them. They were all taller than she was.

"We're here from the state," the man said, superfluously. "I'm Charles Mastrangelo. Is Mother Grey here?"

"I'm Mother Lavinia Grey. Please come in."

They came in. Towser ran out of the kitchen, arched his back, danced on his tiptoes, shivered all over in a paroxysm of unusual friendliness, and weeweed on Mastrangelo's leg. "Pets," he muttered, making a note on his clipboard. As Mother Grey dragged the dog back to the kitchen and closed him in, the inspector said, "You don't mean to have this animal present after the center opens, do you, Reverend Grey?"

"This is my dog," said Mother Grey. "We live here."

"Pets are permitted," one of the women said mildly, as the other one stared at Mastrangelo's wet pant leg.

"If they are effectively controlled," said Mastrangelo, "by leash, command, or cage. In no case are they to be kept in areas used for food preparation. That is the kitchen, isn't it?"

"Yes . . . well . . . I can see that we'll have to make a few changes." They opened the door to the hall closet, and Simon Ratcher's cat came streaking out and tore up the stairs, doing a convincing impersonation of an evil spirit. The inspectors just looked at one another, eyebrows raised. "Now, how do you suppose he got in there?" said Mother Grey.

Testing the foot-candles in obscure corners, counting the bathroom fixtures, measuring the temperature of the hot water (it was supposed to be 110 degrees), muttering things about life safety, making notes, the inspection team went on about their business. Mother Grey followed them around for a while. She had to consciously restrain herself from wringing her hands. *Unprepared.* At last she left them to their work and returned to her office in the undercroft of St. Bede's, there to try to distract her mind somehow.

Her hand almost reached for the drawer holding the envelope with the pictures of the boys. Perhaps if she had a better look at their faces, she might be able to recognize others besides the one she had identified last night. Just in time, she had a vision of the day-care inspection team walking in and catching her with child pornography in her hands. No, no. That would never do.

Then she was going to go get the book of spells that Deedee had left with her and study it carefully, on the chance that it would hold some clue to Ratcher's life and death. No, no. Not to get caught by the day-care inspection team reading a book on Satanism.

So then she thought, *I'll look at Simon Ratcher's address book. Surely I can do that without com-*

promising myself. In the eyes of Mastrangelo and his crew, anyway. If they saw her looking at the thing, they would have no way of knowing it was evidence in a murder case, or that she and another respectable woman of the cloth had lately acquired it in a midnight break-in. To look at it now would be perfectly safe.

The book was bound in brown leather, smooth and warm to the touch, and stamped in gold. The spaces for names and addresses inside were of a good size, as befits a person with early presbyopia. Simon Ratcher had written neatly and clearly. The book was not new but lightly stained with old fingermarks, the entries inscribed in several different colors of ink in several different stages of fading. It was not a loose-leaf book, Mother Grey was almost surprised to note. She realized that she must have formed the impression that the deceased was the sort of fellow who would want to be able rip out the names of his friends and replace them with new ones from time to time according to fashion.

But were these personal or business contacts?

For instance, here was Ellen Warthen's name and number.

Perhaps Ellen planned to get Simon Ratcher to sell her paintings. Did he sell new paintings? Or maybe there was, in fact, something between them. There was a footstep in the hall outside, and Mother Grey jumped up and rushed out to greet the inspection team. Also to keep them out of her office.

"We've seen enough, Reverend Grey," said Mr. Mastrangelo, a remark she found chilling. He handed her several sheets of notebook paper, a list of the deficiencies they had found. "We'll give you a detailed report later," he said. "This will give you something to go on for now."

"Thank you." She walked up the steps with them into the yard, willing their attention away from the bottom drawer of her desk.

Suddenly Mastrangelo noticed Lord Bountiful's latest gift gathering another blanket of snow in the side yard. "What's that?" he said.

"It seems to be a freezer," Mother Grey admitted. Oh, Lord, the cats. She had forgotten all about them in her terror of having the inspectors find the pictures. *Let him not open the freezer,* she prayed.

"I hope you realize it will have to be removed before the child-care center can begin operations."

"We'll be sure to take care of it," said Mother Grey.

Each of them gave her a dead-fish handshake. "We'll be back next week to see it before you open," said Mastrangelo. Then they all piled into the state car. As they drove away in the general direction of Trenton, the snow turned back to freezing rain again.

The cats. Something would have to be done.

The problem of the cats, as Mother Grey saw it, was twofold. The first and most urgent aspect was the problem of what to do with them. She could advertise for their owners in the paper. That way whoever the cats belonged to could come and claim them, give them a decent burial, and undergo a healing process of grief. Then with the cats out of the way, she could dispose of the freezer as seemed most expedient. This seemed like an attractive option until she visualized how it would play out, the line of bereaved children and old women stretching around the church, the momentous flinging open of the freezer lid, the howls of dismay as Fluffy's body was identified, the little girls weeping, the old folks having their heart attacks.

Or the cats could be quietly buried. She could get Ralph to do it. But, no, Ralph was in jail. Schwartz, maybe. Did Schwartz owe her any favors? She might bring up the subject of burying the cats while she was interviewing him about Ralph's whereabouts and state of mind on the morning of the murder, something she had to do anyway—it was on her list. But no, the ground was frozen too hard for burying things. Even if it weren't, to disturb the earth anywhere in town while the police were still looking for body parts would probably be a mistake. It would only confuse things.

What would be the most open, honest way to deal with the cats without having to deal with their next of kin? She could call the animal control officer.

The animal control officer was Dr. Sheila Dresner, the town veterinarian, a good friend of Mother Grey's. She telephoned her at once and explained the situation. Sheila made her tell the whole inside story of the murder, at which she was suitably agog, before getting down to brass tacks.

"So what you want me to do is . . ." she prompted.

". . . to take the bodies away and handle the notification of the owners," said Mother Grey cheerfully, trusting that the matter would now be taken out of her hands.

"But where did they come from?"

"Ah. I don't really know."

"From what you're saying, it seems almost as though the cats are some kind of evidence in the murder investigation."

"I guess they might be."

"If that's the case, Vinnie, you need to speak to the county prosecutor's office before you do anything with them at all, or the freezer either."

More delays. "Horrors."

"Call me back after you talk to the investigating officers," her friend said. "But I can't believe Dave didn't explain all this to you."

"Dave hasn't been available this week to advise me."

"What's up?"

"He's in Boston burying Felicia's mother."

"For a week? Roman Catholic funerals must be really something." Mother Grey received this in silence. "Well, I suppose the ground is frozen pretty hard up there. Probably it takes them a week to dig a hole." Still Mother Grey said nothing, and at last Sheila perceived, even over the telephone, that Mother Grey was not happy. "Something is wrong between you, isn't it?"

"I think he wants to go back to Felicia," said Mother Grey.

"How do you feel about that?"

"Awful," she admitted. "But I can get along without Dave Dogg."

"I told you you should have married him the first time he asked you."

She sighed. "Well, you know what they say, Sheila. Men are like streetcars."

"So they tell me. But when was the last time you saw a streetcar?"

So Sheila was able to give her no help with the cats. Of course, if they were evidence in Simon Ratcher's murder investigation, then it would be up to the police to haul the freezer away, cats and all. But would they do this before the day-care center was to open?

If the cats were evidence. Mother Grey thought they were. But what made her think so?

How had they gotten into the freezer? That was the second aspect of the cat problem; Sheila had put her finger right on it. As far as Mother Grey was aware, she herself had the only key. The locked freezer hadn't been opened by her since Chip and Lance Sedgewick delivered it to St. Bede's. Therefore the cats had to have been in the freezer when they brought it here.

So where had the freezer come from?

It was time to have a talk with Rodman Sedge-wick.

Surprisingly, Ouida herself answered the tel-ephone on the third ring. Must be the maid's day off. Roddy wasn't home, she said. "Is there any-thing I can help you with, Mother Grey?" Her tone was frosty. Mother Grey remembered how she had swooped down on her husband while they were talking at the reception. Insanely jealous. Certainly insane to think that Mother Grey had any designs on her self-important windbag of a spouse. Even if he weren't so unpleasant (and of course married), he was much too tall to be inter-esting.

"I'm calling about the freezer," Mother Grey said.

"Freezer?"

"Chip and Lance brought a freezer to St. Bede's on Sunday," said Mother Grey. "I'm very anxious to find out exactly where it came from. Was it part of your household, Mrs. Sedgewick, or—"

"I'm afraid I don't know anything about it, Mother Grey. Our freezer is still right where it's been for the last ten years or so. If you like I'll ask Lance and Chip when they come home."

"Please do that, Mrs. Sedgewick."

Was it time to go over there and snoop?

Or was it not rather time to apply herself to the list of deficiencies that the child-care facility inspectors had found, with a view to getting the place up and running by a week from Monday?

The list was very long.

The nickel-and-dime stuff was daunting enough, but the most serious problems were what they called life safety concerns, which included things like emergency exits that had to be located diagonally opposite the main entrance, a ramp suitable for wheeling cribs out the door in case of fire, and a brand-new fire escape that had to come from the upper floors all the way to the ground and rest on a patch of land that the church didn't even own. Major structural changes. Land acquisition.

She began trying to estimate the cost of correcting each item, starting with the least expensive. When the total reached fifty thousand dollars, and that was pretty soon, she sat back and groaned. *This time, Vinnie*, she said to herself, *you've bitten off more than you can chew.*

Nevertheless she decided to go and talk to her next-door neighbor about buying or renting the square of land in question. The Lord might provide the money. You never knew.

Octogenarian Horace Burkhardt was an old friend and breakfast companion of Mother Grey's. On pleasant mornings they often met for coffee and doughnuts at Delio's, where he filled her in on the news of the town (mostly fifty-year-old news, since that was what Horace remembered best). She hadn't seen anything of the old man since the weather got so bad; she supposed he was staying indoors to keep from falling down and breaking a hip. He had a daughter nearby who did his shopping and took care of him.

Horace was a great benefactor of St. Bede's, although not a parishioner. When the old rectory burned down, he let Mother Grey live in one of his houses rent free until the insurance check cleared, and then he sold the house to the church for a very reasonable price, whereupon it became St. Bede's new rectory. In view of his past generosity, Mother Grey thought perhaps he would be moved to donate the little patch of land to the day-care center. One could always hope.

Horace was at home when she rang the bell next door. The old man shuffled to the door and opened it. Mother Grey thought he looked unwell; his eyes were bloodshot; his normally pink nose was stoplight red and runny. He was clutching several sweaters around his stooped shoulders. The sweaters were not new. They bore signs of wear and abusive treatment by moths.

"Horace! I hope you aren't sick."

"Sick of winter," the old man said. "Think I'll go to Florida."

"Sounds wonderful."

"What can I do for you, Mother Vinnie?"

"I guess you can sell me some land."

"You want to buy my land?"

"A little square patch of it on the north side of the rectory."

"What do you want it for? Come in. Sit down. I'll make you coffee."

She stepped into the house. It was very like the rectory itself, laid out similarly, built around the same time of the same materials. This house, however, still had the same furniture and wall-paper that Horace and his bride had installed when they were newlyweds. The only items that appeared to have been added since then were the television and the many-jointed plastic-covered lounge chair where Horace spent much of his time. Mother Grey perched on the chintz-covered sofa. "No coffee for me, thanks," she said. "I only wanted to talk to you about my troubles with the state child-care facility inspectors."

"What's the problem?" asked Horace as he sank back into his lounge chair and adjusted the angle of recline.

"It's about a fire escape for the child-care center," she said. "They say it needs to come down the north side of the rectory and rest on the ground. As you know, our property line is right up next to the house."

"And you want to buy the land underneath it."

"I guess I need to."

Horace pushed himself back in his lounge chair and sighed, a wistful sort of sigh. "This winter really has me beat," he said.

"Don't tell me a little thing like the weather could get an old campaigner like you down."

"Down? No, I'm never down. But I have made a tough decision, something I've been thinking about for a long time."

"What's that?"

"I've decided to go and live with my other daughter in Florida."

"Oh, Horace! We'll miss you so! Delio's won't be the same."

"It means I need to sell this house. Not a little patch out of the backyard, but the whole thing."

"I see."

With a sinking heart, she heard him say, "I could let you have it for a hundred and fifty thousand dollars."

12

The difficulties of starting a day-care center were apparently insurmountable. Mother Grey decided that a mere murder investigation was a trifle. Anyway, a good walk would clear her head. After parting with Horace, she put on her coat and went over to the Fairview to find out what Saraleigh knew about the murder, if anything.

For instance, what was it that made her think Rex would no longer bother her?

Freddy answered the door. The sound of the television rolled out the door and over Mother Grey, along with the smell of garlic and cabbage, and she realized she had forgotten to eat lunch. It was two o'clock already. But what was Freddy doing home?

"Why aren't you in school, young man?" she asked him.

"We got another snow day," he said.

"Really? You'll be going to school all summer long to make them up."

"Yeah, well . . ."

The future never comes when you're nine. *Summer? What summer?* "Where's your mother?"

"She went to the hospital."

"Good heavens. Is she all right?"

"Yeah, it was about a job."

"Doing what?"

"I think she said delivering meal trays and stuff. She's having an interview, she said."

"Who will mind the girls while she's at work?"

"You will. Right? Aren't you going to have a day-care center?"

"Of course," said Mother Grey. *If only I can find two hundred thousand dollars.*

"She said the job doesn't pay much, but the benefits are good. She said I'm supposed to take care of the babies till she gets back."

"Can you do that? Will you be all right?"

"Sure."

"How long will she be gone, do you think?"

"Another hour or two."

"I'll come back later, then."

"Okay."

But she never did go back; after she got home, Mother Grey fed the dog and cat and fell into an exhausted sleep. By the time she woke up, it was too late in the evening for decently visiting.

* * *

When Freddy Kane woke up next morning, his mother told him they were having school. "But there's still snow outside," he said.

"Doesn't matter," she said. "Get going." He got up and washed and dressed and ate. On his way out the door, his mom reminded him about his coat and his backpack, so he grabbed them and took off.

He decided to take a detour around by the river to see how the ice was doing. Then there was a velociraptor chasing him, and he had to go along by hiding in all the bushes.

By and by, he came to a little hole in the snow behind one of the bushes, about big enough for a small animal or something, and he looked into it because it might be something cool, a rabbit or whatever. But it wasn't an animal. It was something even cooler. It was a gun.

He put his bare hand in the snow (he had lost his gloves last week, or maybe it was the week before) and pulled out a freezing-cold revolver, a big thing too heavy for him even to aim. It was real. It seemed to have real bullets. He thought about using it to shoot at the velociraptor, but since that wasn't real, it didn't seem right.

What to do with it? He could use it to kill Rex, if Ralph hadn't killed Rex already. He could take it to school and show it to all his friends, if he wouldn't get expelled for bringing a gun to school. Or he could take it to the cops and get them to pay him money for it. He heard someplace that if you took guns to the police station, the cops would pay you.

Through the window he saw Officer Jimmy Finn talking on the phone. He went down the steps and into the police station swinging the gun by the trigger guard. Officer Finn looked up when he dropped the gun on the counter. It was really heavy. Freddy was glad to put it down.

Officer Finn said, "Talk to you later, Rose," and hung up the phone. His expression as he looked at the gun was one of intense interest. "What's this, little buddy?" he said.

"I heard you were giving money for guns," Freddy said. "Here's a gun for you."

"I hadn't heard we were giving money for guns," the policeman said. "I think that was in the city. Looks like a .357 Magnum. Where did you get this?"

"In the bushes down by the river." Was he going to pay him for it or not? It was time for Freddy to be at school. Already the crossing guard would be gone, and he would have to get across the highway by himself, with all those speeding gravel trucks.

"It's loaded too," Officer Finn murmured. "You did right, son. Only next time leave the gun where you find it and give us a call."

"I don't find guns all that often."

"I'm glad to hear it."

"Do I get any money?"

"Sure," said Finn, reaching into his own pocket. "Here's five dollars."

"Awesome." Freddy took the money and rushed out of the police station. With five dollars he could buy a lot of candy, maybe some baseball cards.

Watching the boy go, Finn had mixed feelings. Now he would have to make out a report on this damned gun.

Loaded, but not fully loaded. One round had been fired. Using a pencil in the trigger guard to avoid smudging fingerprints—a totally useless precaution, probably, but you never knew—Finn picked up the gun and sniffed the barrel. Judging by the smell, he would say it had been fired recently.

Just then Chief Harry came out of his office and caught him smelling the gun. "The hell you doing, Jim?" he said.

"A kid just brought this in," Finn said. "He found it by the river. I think it might have been fired within the last day or so."

" 'Zat so?" said Chief Harry. "Interesting. Looks an awful lot like that piece that we used to keep in the evidence closet. I don't suppose you got a name and address on that kid."

"It's that kid, you know. He's always running around the streets. Kreevitch knows who he is."

"I bet Kreevitch knows a lot of stuff," said Chief Harry. "Maybe we can get him to share it with us."

"This ain't evidence in the case of the headless body, is it?" Finn said.

"I hope to Christ it ain't," said the chief. He unlocked the evidence closet, checked the shelves, and began to curse in a low voice. Finn concluded that the other gun wasn't in there, that this was probably the same gun, and that as a result they were going to have to take more shit from the county prosecutor's office.

Ash Wednesday at St. Dinarius. Father Bingley always did noonday prayers. As usual, he expected only a handful of old ladies (not unlike Mother Grey's congregation on a good Sunday), since the press of business affairs took most of St. Dinarius's parishioners out of town in the middle of a weekday. To his surprise and pleasure, however, what should he see among the withered countenances of the usual widows but the well-greased face of Rodman Sedgewick.

Father Bingley was even more delighted when Sedgewick, senatorial hopeful and St. Dinarius's richest and most powerful parishioner, approached him after the service and asked to speak to him in private.

It was so seldom that the up-and-coming politician had time for him these days. The hurly-burly of the great building drive, where Rodman Sedgewick had offered so much generous help, was over. These days the congregation seemed to fit nicely into the current facilities. *Maybe even a little loosely,* Father Bingley said uneasily to himself. A few more families had left last month. It was difficult even for a prosperous parish like St. Dinarius to thrive in these godless times, with their overpowering worldy influences.

It might even be that St. Dinarius needed some sort of spiritual shot in the arm. Father Bingley prayed for guidance in this matter, but all he could see was Mother Grey, hanging on for dear life at St. Bede's in Fishersville, even gaining an inch now and then, using the church to further her peculiar social agenda. Women priests! An oxymoron. Our Lord's apostles were all men, and so should be his priests. If only Mother Grey would consent to close the church in Fishersville and pursue some more fitting line of endeavor! He wanted the windows of St. Bede's for his own St. Dinarius, where they could be properly maintained and cared for. He wanted her brass Communion rail with its ivy leaves. He even wanted her minuscule congregation, except of course for the rattiest ones, those disgraceful characters who were always getting into trouble with the law. Old Delight van Buskirk would be an ornament to the parish of St. Dinarius. A lovely woman, Mrs. van Buskirk had gone to school with Father Bingley's mother and reminded him of her in many ways. Father Bingley missed his mother. It was scarcely six months since she had gone to her reward.

But Lavinia Grey was so stubborn. She refused to loosen her grip on what she considered to be her own. And in St. Bede's, the parish she gripped so tightly, Father Rupert Bingley was beginning to recognize a tiny spark, a spark he coveted even more than he coveted the appointments of her beautiful and decaying old church.

Father Bingley hung up his vestments and made his way down the hallway to his private office in the adjoining parish house, a useful and good building constructed almost entirely with the aid of Rodman Sedgewick's generous donations. He found his benefactor waiting for him at the office door. He unlocked it, and they went in.

The view from Rupert Bingley's walnut-paneled private office was almost as good as the view from the church steps, which took in the entire borough of Rolling Hills. Right across the street was the rectory. If he looked carefully, Bingley could look through his own kitchen window and see his dear wife preparing lunch, something special for the first day of Lent—low-cholesterol fish, probably. Martha was extremely conscientious about his diet. It occurred to Bingley, with the fleeting sensation of a rabbit walking on his grave, that Rodman Sedgewick had come to collect a debt, the unspoken quid pro quo that Bingley owed him for financing the parish house and this excellent office. It was true that most of those who gave large sums of money to the church expected to collect their reward in the hereafter. Bingley suspected that Rodman Sedgewick was of a more worldly disposition than that.

He hoped he would not be asked to preach from the pulpit on some political topic.

But Sedgewick's request proved to be something completely unexpected. "You're on the Department of Missions, isn't that right, Father?"

"Yes," said Bingley. "I have that honor. It's a great deal of work, but I feel that if my services can be of use to the Diocese of New Jersey, why then—"

"Ouida and I have been discussing the plight of working mothers in this county."

"You have?" Bingley tried to picture Ouida Sedgewick and her husband sitting around the fireplace feeling sorry for working mothers while their maid refilled the Scotch glasses. It was a strange picture. Ouida, he knew for a fact, had never worked a day in her life, except as a volunteer in a number of worthy causes.

"Yes," Rodman Sedgewick went on, "we feel that what is needed is more day care, and we're willing to back that up with a contribution of two hundred thousand dollars."

"Ah!" Bingley put his hand to his heart. What a surprise! Instead of collecting a debt, this good and generous man had come to the church to offer more. Perhaps this was the shot in the arm that St. Dinarius needed, a project for the community! Father Bingley understood that many of the wives and mothers of Rolling Hills were out working these days, although he was under the impression that they all had nannies. "The bishop will be so pleased," he said. "With that kind of money, we can begin a needs-assessment study right away—"

"I understand that Mother Lavinia Grey is

starting a child-care facility in Fishersville that's meant to serve families in the entire area. Correct me if I'm wrong."

Mother Grey? Is this about helping Mother Grey? "I had heard of some such thing," said Bingley. "Of course, dear Mother Grey always has so many irons in the fire. But the diocese—"

"I was told that this child-care center was due to open a week from next Monday. Ouida and I were very excited to hear this. But then they told me that it might be delayed, that Mother Grey was taking up her valuable time with some murder investigation."

"Strange case," said Bingley. "They found a headless corpse." *More stupidness in Fishersville. What a place. Certainly the Episcopal Church as he knew it had no business there.*

"Has she found out anything?" said Sedgewick.

"I have no idea. But you're right. It's not her proper area of concern."

"The children of Greater Fishersville are more important, Father Bingley. I'll tell you what to do. Go to her and offer her this money in the name of the diocese. Tell her the two hundred thousand is hers if she can really start a child-care center in two weeks. Don't mention our names; Ouida and I really don't want any credit."

Bingley thought, *Greater Fishersville?* He said, "I'm sure she can open her child-care center in two weeks, with the help of the diocese, of course. Caring for children is such a womanly activity. I'm quite certain it will take all her time and attention."

"Of course. With her off the case, the police can get on with their prosecution of that person—what's his name?"

"Voercker, Ralph Voercker. I think she wants to protect him because he's one of her vestrymen. Hopelessly insane, but our dear Lavinia is such a mother hen."

"Sad case," said Sedgewick.

"Sad," Bingley agreed. "And such a waste of time for a woman of the cloth to try to do the job of the police, when there's work enough in the church to keep her busy." His heart was a lump of lead in his breast. For a fleeting moment, he had had a vision of a great new mission for St. Dinarius, a whole new way to carry the banner of Jesus Christ into the twenty-first century. Outreach! But the banner was to be handed to his rival in Fishersville.

It's such a waste of time for a woman of the cloth to try to do the job of the police, said Mother Grey to herself. Nevertheless, if the police were content to think Ralph was guilty, what else could she do but try to find out the truth herself? Next on her list of tasks was interviewing Ralph's friends, the disturbed young men. Naturally their telephone line was still busy. Schwartz spent his entire life on the Internet these days. Mother Grey was beginning to wonder whether it was entirely healthy for him.

In the halfway house, Danny Handleman came up out of the cellar and charged up the back stairs, waving a pair of camouflage-printed trousers in one hand and a wad of soggy greenbacks in the other. There was blood in his eye.

"Schwartz!"

"I'm online," Schwartz called from behind his closed door. "Whaddaya want now?"

"We have to have a house meeting," Danny shouted. "You have transgressed, big time."

"Oh, shit," Danny heard him muttering, but he was not deterred. This time he knew he was on unassailably superior moral ground.

Presently Schwartz came out of his room. "Your underwear is dirty," Danny observed.

"If you'd do the laundry a little faster, I'd put on clean underwear," said Schwartz.

"Funny you should mention the laundry," Danny said. "Tell me something. Do you remember how many times we've agreed to empty our pockets before putting our clothes in the hamper?"

"I suppose you're trying to make some sort of point."

"Maybe you'd like to tell me what this is," Danny said, and flourished the wad of bills.

Schwartz's jaw dropped. Clearly he had forgotten putting the money in his pocket. "Give me that," he said.

"I'm not sure it's really yours," said Danny.

"Maybe I'll give it to you if you can tell me how much is here."

"Ten thousand dollars."

"Where did you get this money, Schwartz?"

"That's my business."

"Have you been dealing drugs or something? You know, I don't want to live in a house where drugs are dealt. I could get in a whole lot of trouble, even go to jail. The police could round me up in a drug bust. If I thought something like that was going on, I would have to go to Mother Grey and ask her to help me find somewhere else to live."

"It's nothing like that. You know I don't deal drugs. Do you ever see any junkies around here?"

"Well, what is this money?"

"My aunt died and left it to me."

"Try again."

"I took it off Rex Perskie."

"You what!"

"There was this bulge in his pocket. I couldn't let all that cash go in the river."

"I can't believe what I'm hearing. First you suborn Ralph Voercker to murder this man, he's probably going to be executed, and then you loot the dead body. I thought you were a better person than that, Schwartz."

"I never looked at it that way. I was thinking in terms of recycling."

"You can't keep it, you know."

"What do you mean, I can't keep it?" said Schwartz.

Danny said, "You can't keep it. It's wrong to rob the dead."

"Well, what do you want me do do, then? Throw it in the river?" There was a knock at the front door.

"We'll talk about this later," said Danny.

Mother Grey scraped the snow off her boots on the boys' front step. The sidewalk in front of the halfway house was under two feet of snow, a lumpy heap that must have slid off the roof in the night. Hers were the first footprints of the morning. Danny answered the door in his robe and pajamas. He seemed surprised to see her. "Mother Vinnie!"

"You boys had better get out here and shovel that walk again. If you don't, the city will make you pay a fine," she said to him.

"Yes, ma'am. Right away."

"May I come in?"

"Oh. Sure. Sure."

He opened the door. The steamy hall smelled a little more neglected than usual. Mother Grey seemed to detect a breakdown in the boys' social order. "Did you put the garbage out yesterday?" she said.

"Schwartz was supposed to," said Danny. "It was his day."

"That doesn't matter, Danny. If you see something that needs doing as badly as that, you should just do it."

"Yes, ma'am. I've been doing . . . doing the laundry."

"Where is Schwartz?"

"He's in his room. Maybe he'll come out later."

"Is he staying in there all the time again? You should have called me."

"It was all his fault," said Danny. "Schwartz was to blame for the whole thing."

"To blame for what whole thing?" Danny just stared at her, blinking a couple of times. "What was his fault?" she said.

"I had nothing to do with it" was all the reply he made.

The smell was really bad. What if the agency did a spot inspection? "Danny, for heaven's sake, wash these dishes. Your house smells awful. You'll be having bugs and rats in here."

"Yes, ma'am."

"Tell Schwartz I want to see him right now."

"Yes, ma'am."

She went to hang up her coat and found that the coat tree that usually stood in the hall was missing. "Where's the coat tree?" she said.

"They left it in the living room, I think."

"Who did?"

"Ralph and Schwartz. None of this had anything to do with me," said Danny.

The living room was a terrible shambles. The coat tree in question lay in splinters in the corner of the room. "Well. This is nice. How do you boys expect to hang up your coats?"

"We're sorry."

"The least you could do is sweep it up."

"Yes, ma'am."

"Danny, I came here to talk to you about Ralph."

"Ralph Voercker," said Danny, with a blank look.

"What was he doing on Monday?"

"He's in trouble, isn't he?"

"Ralph is in jail, Danny. They think he killed somebody."

"I would never go to jail," Danny said. "If I killed somebody, I would just hop a train and leave town. They wouldn't ever catch me. I would assume a new identity in another town and live under a false name."

"If you hopped a train in Fishersville, you wouldn't get any farther than the county seat," Mother Grey pointed out. "It's a hobby train, just for tourists."

"I could do that," Danny said. "Nobody knows me in the county seat."

"Do you believe Ralph killed somebody?"

"It was all Schwartz's doing."

"What was?"

"Oh, nothing." He began to whistle.

Something was going on here. But what? She would never know if she waited for Danny to tell her. Perhaps she could browbeat Schwartz until he came clean. "Go and tell Schwartz I want to see him *right now*."

"Yes, ma'am," said Danny. He went upstairs to call Schwartz.

She puttered around, straightening up a little, waiting for Schwartz to make himself decent.

In less than five minutes Schwartz came pounding down the stairs, dressed in fatigues, his dark hair all awry. His eyes were wild and his whiskers were several days old, but oddly enough, Schwartz did not look like a man with a guilty secret. Not exactly. A man having a manic episode, perhaps.

"Mother Vinnie! I'm so glad you came over! Wow, this is such a great coincidence. I have all this stuff for you." He carried a manila envelope fat with computer printouts.

"Schwartz, I want you to tell me everything you know about Ralph," said Mother Grey.

"Ralph Voercker?"

"Yes, Ralph Voercker. What was he doing on Monday?"

"Nothing that I know of. Was he doing something on Monday? Look, this is all my correspondence with the Satanism and Sorcery bulletin board."

"Did you see Ralph on Monday?"

"Well, yeah. He spent Sunday night here. Is Ralph in some kind of trouble? He's in some kind of trouble, isn't he? I wish I could be of help to him somehow."

"I think you can. Tell me what Ralph was doing on Monday morning."

"Well, he . . . he slept late, and then he had French toast for breakfast, and then he just kind of hung around the house all morning until he went out and the police arrested him for nothing."

"What happened to the coat tree?" said Mother Grey, taking a different tack.

"Harmless horseplay," said Schwartz. "What did Ralph tell you?"

"I can't say I've discussed it with him."

"Well, what did Dan say?"

"He seemed to think you were up to no good."

"Just a little harmless horseplay. You know Danny. He thinks ill of everything. But look at this."

"You didn't go anywhere with Ralph Monday morning? Or see where he went and what he did?"

Schwartz appeared to search his mind for a moment, or maybe he was taking time to compose a good lie. His gaze shifted to the lower left for an instant, a sure sign of creative activity. "What did Fred tell you?" he asked, meeting her gaze.

"Nothing at all. What is there to tell? Does Freddy know something I should know?"

"Oh, no. Nothing. So here's what I found, Mother Vinnie. You've got to see this. I've been on the Internet for days."

She gave up and took the folder from him. Maybe later she could brush up on her interrogation techniques. If Dave ever came back, he could give her some pointers. She let Schwartz ramble on about his discoveries.

"Your so-called Clavicles of Solomon are pretty disgusting," he said. "Some kid who calls himself Devil Boy uploaded a spell called the Hand of Glory. Why Glory I don't know. Take a look at it." He took the folder back and withdrew a couple of pages. "Here," he said.

She glanced over it, took in the part about cutting off the hand of a hanged felon, then came to the bit where the grease has to be cooked out of it. Hoping she didn't look as sick as she felt, she put the pages back. "Edifying," she said. "Is this one of the Clavicles of Solomon?"

"I told you they were disgusting, Mother Vinnie," said Schwartz.

13

At the Ash Wednesday evening Mass, Mother Grey had to carry on all by herself, since one of her acolytes was in jail and the other one simply didn't turn up. Where was Edward? With a family situation as unstable as the Warthen's was turning out to be, he could be anywhere. Poor kid.

Mother Grey took one last good breath of the sweet beeswax candle smell she loved so well. The lights were out. Everything was put away in its place. St. Bede's was set for the night. She made her way out through the sacristy, locking the outside door securely behind her.

Before she went home to her bed, she would look in on Edward. It wasn't all that late. Maybe he was sick. Maybe he forgot. Or maybe he was in some kind of trouble.

The major himself answered the door. He carried a drink in one hand and leaned on the door frame. His glasses were down on the end of his nose. Something about him reminded her of the tweedy boys she used to like when she was in college.

"I'm glad you're here, Vinnie," he said.

"I came to see whether you were all okay," she said.

"Not as okay as we could be. We're having a hard time with this." He put his arm around her, took her hand, and held it. "You're an awfully nice woman." Brandy breath. He must have found a replacement for the despoiled bottle.

She disengaged herself and pushed past him to come inside. "Edward wasn't in church tonight," she said. "Is he here?"

"I haven't seen him since he left for school this morning," the major said. "He never came home."

"My word! Do you think you should tell the police he's missing?"

"I did tell them. I called about an hour ago. They are assuming he ran away."

"It's awfully cold for a little young boy to be out," said Mother Grey. Edward, so slightly built, would be easy prey to hypothermia. "What about his friend Adam? Maybe he's at his house. Have you talked to his family?"

"My dear, I don't even know the child's last name."

"How can this be?"

"My . . . wife . . . kept track of these household details. I believe she knew the boy's mother." He was slurring his words a bit. Cold unease stole into Mother Grey's vitals. Drunk, the boy on the street somewhere . . .

"What about Ellen, then? He could have gone to be with her. Have you found out where she is yet?"

"No."

"I see." She stood staring disapproval at him until he began to squirm uncomfortably.

"She did leave a note," he said at last. "Do you want to see it?"

She knew how improper it would be for her to look at private correspondence between Ellen Warthen and her husband. It was not her business. Yet if she didn't look at the note and see for herself that Ellen really meant to leave, satisfy herself that she left under her own power . . . Mother Grey might think that the major had . . . "Yes, please."

The note was folded in three and stuck under a vase on the mantelpiece. The major took it and handed it to her. It was written in Ellen's boxy, clearly legible hand, blue fountain-pen ink on creamy vellum note paper:

I have to get away for a while to try to sort out my life. You know how difficult things have been between us. Don't try to follow me.

No clue as to how to reach her. "And did you try to follow her?"

"Of course I tried to follow her. I called all her usual haunts. I even got in touch with her art friends. Nobody knows where she is. You know, Vinnie, Ellen hasn't been much of a wife to me these past few years. It isn't much different, whether she's home or she isn't home. Elmina keeps the house clean, Edward keeps to himself." He took a couple of steps toward her, invading her personal space. "I'm a lonely man."

She stepped back. She noticed a smear of earth on the pale gray rug. She thought, *Dog footprint*, then realized that the Warthens owned no animals.

Suddenly Mother Grey realized Ellen's note wasn't dated. Maybe the Major had saved it from one of the other times she left him. Maybe there had been no note this time.

So why is there dirt on the floor? Why now? Everything is frozen. One of those unwelcome mental pictures appeared to her of the slender major, in her fantasy wearing his dress uniform, a long pale beam of winter sunlight slanting through the cellar window to illuminate his chiseled features, digging up the earth under the Wagonner mansion to bury his wife.

And maybe his son as well. Mother Grey edged toward the door. When he followed her, she shook his hand and promised to pray for him. Then as soon as she was out of sight of the house, she ran all the way home like a terrified child. *This is good exercise*, she told herself. *Clears the brain*.

But it didn't, and she slept badly.

* * *

Since it was Lent, there had to be morning Mass, even on Thursday, though hardly anyone came. When it was over, she went to her office and revised her list of pertinent questions, writing down the things that really puzzled her, not just the things that she thought would help her solve the case.

1. *Where is Edward?*
2. *What happened to Ellen Warthen?*
3. *Where did the dead cats come from?*
4. *What makes Saraleigh think she's safe from Rex?*
5. *When would be a good time to put the evidence back in S.R.'s apartment?*

The phone rang. She grabbed for it, thinking it might be Edward, but it was Ouida Sedgewick.

"I asked the boys this morning about the freezer, Mother Grey. They said they picked it up from Ellen's garage."

"Ellen Warthen?"

"I don't know whether she told you, but she was converting her garage into a painting studio. There were some large things she needed to get rid of in order to make some room. Evidently one of them was the freezer."

"So the freezer belonged to the Warthens."

"I think so. Last Sunday, Chip and Lance took Roddy's truck to Fishersville to give her some help disposing of things. Roddy told them to take the freezer to St. Bede's."

Mother Grey thanked her and hung up, her mind reeling. Ellen Warthen? Fifteen cats? She called the Warthen household to demand an explanation, but there was no answer.

But then, Ellen Warthen wasn't at home, was she? She had run off someplace, possibly to an expensive hotel in New York City.

According to her husband.

She called Saraleigh. The phone was still out of service.

She called the county prosecutor's office and left a message for the detective in charge of the Ratcher case to call her back. She made a note to tell him about the cats; perhaps he would haul them away. She thought of telling him everything else that was on her mind. "Armstrong Warthen has murdered his wife, his son, and fifteen cats. Look for the bodies of the humans in his cellar." It sounded crazy in the light of day, and it would continue to sound crazy even after sundown.

To think that she had run in fear from the stiff. Nuts to this. What she needed to do was to inspect the Warthens' cellar. A good look in the windows would probably suffice. With her trusty flashlight she would have nothing to fear from the major; if he tried to murder her, too, she could simply bat him over the head with it. It was time to gird her loins, take the bull by the horns, and beard the lion in his den.

* * *

Saraleigh came to see Ralph at the Blue Roof Hotel. The guard told him he could have a couple of minutes' visiting time but no touching. That was okay; he didn't feel comfortable getting close to her. He felt as if he needed a bath, and his breath smelled of jail food.

After they greeted each other, she told him the bad news.

"I got fired from my job at the hospital, Ralphie."

"You got a job?" he said.

"Whatsa matter, you think I can't hold a job?"

"But what about the babies?"

"Mother Grey is starting a day-care center," Saraleigh said. "They'll be fine."

"Oh. Right." Mother Grey would save them again. "But you said you got fired."

She sighed. "For a while yesterday morning it was going okay. I was supposed to deliver the food trays to the patients on this one floor, and it was going fine. They gave me this big cart, and I went down the hall giving the lunches to first this one and then that one.

"Then I came to this room where there's a patient asleep in the corner. I got the orders mixed up, and I was going to give him lunch. They said don't give him lunch, he's in a coma and can't eat. So I looked, and it was Rex, and I dropped the tray."

"Rex."

"Yeah."

"He's alive."

"Barely."

Ralph scratched his beard. A sensation of lightness slowly came over him, starting from somewhere around his solar plexus and spreading upward through his shoulders and neck. So he hadn't murdered Rex after all. "I'm sort of glad, honey, you know? I don't really like the idea of killing people."

"I don't mind the idea," she said with a faraway look. "Maybe I'll do it myself next time."

"So they fired you?"

"They said it was for dropping food all over the other patient."

"It's too bad."

"Yeah, well. I guess I'm not cut out to be a tray deliverer."

"We'll be okay. You can type, right? We don't have to kill people to get along, Saraleigh."

"I hope you can get out of here before Saturday," she said. "I want us to get married."

As Mother Grey crouched beside his basement window, playing a flashlight across his furnace, awnings, and window screens, with a quick look on the side at his washer and dryer, the major came out into the yard unexpectedly (how else?) and discovered her. Heaven knew what he thought of the edifying rear view of her burglar sweatpants. "Can I help you with something?" he said.

A beat of silence while she searched for a good lie. First stealing, now lying—she was sinking deeper and deeper into iniquity. "I dropped my contact lens," she said at last. "I thought it might have rolled over here into the window well." The major looked puzzled. "I thought if I used this flashlight, I could see it by the gleam," she added lamely.

"Let me help you look," said the major. He hunkered down in the snow with her. They felt all around, Mother Grey growing more and more uncomfortable. He seemed to be perfectly sober.

Perhaps she had wronged this man. The cursory inspection of the cellar floor she had been able to make before getting caught had shown it to be solid concrete. No dirt for burying. The major began to shiver. He was dressed for the indoors in a blue cardigan sweater. His slim freckled hand trembled as he poked the snowy leaves.

Pretending to wrap something in her handkerchief, she cried, "Here it is, I've got it!" They both got stiffly to their feet.

"Come indoors," he said. "It's cold out here." She went inside, but only as far as the foyer. Ellen's paintings stared at them, lush hairy flowers in beautiful urns.

"Do you have any news of Ellen or Edward?" she asked.

"No," he said. "Nothing."

"I thought perhaps I could help you look for Edward."

"If you can help, I would be very grateful. I don't know what to do," he said.

"Do you want to come along? We could try the schoolyard, the pizza parlor, the usual hangouts. Maybe someone has seen him."

"Thanks. I'd like that." He got his coat.

As they headed for the local pizzeria, she thought, *He might have dug up the floor and then put new concrete over the graves.* But it seemed unlikely. His hands (still gloveless in the cold) were perfectly smooth and well manicured—hardly the hands of a man who had recently done some serious digging. In any case, no matter what he might have to cover up, the image of Major Armstrong Warthen soiling his aristocratic hands with concrete was simply not credible.

This was not to say she trusted him.

They looked in a number of possible kid hangouts around town: the pizza parlor, the schoolyard, the library. Nobody they talked to had seen Edward or his friend Adam, or even seemed to know who they were. Then on a side street of town, they came across a small shop that seemed to be for the exchange of video games. It looked like a likely place to find kids, so they went in.

It was dark inside. What light there was came from two pinball machines that no one was playing and from a lighted display case of used video games. A clerk lurked in the shadows behind the counter, an unhealthy-looking young man with his hair in a ponytail.

On the floor in the middle of the shop sat three boys of about fourteen or fifteen. For a moment Mother Grey thought that one of them might be Edward's friend Adam. Then she thought, no, but perhaps those boys in the pictures—

The three affected the same style as Adam; indeed, they resembled him and also one another, the way brothers might, with their fair skin, incipient beards, and occasional pimples. There was a roundness to their flesh, not fat exactly but a well-nourished quality that was not muscular. Their hair was straight and greasy and of a color that in a woman would be called mousy brown, worn in bizarre haircuts, shaved for the most part, with long hanks here and there falling shoulder-length or into their faces.

They were leafing through albums of cards, ring binders with plastic card-holder inserts such as collectors use. The cards that so held their interest might have been playing cards, except that instead of hearts, clubs, spades, and diamonds they were decorated with ugly brown monsters and strange symbols. They glanced briefly at the intruder grown-ups and continued their play, which seemed to be trading and discussing the cards.

"I can let you have these two for the spell of invisibility," one of them said.

"Give me your cacadaemon, and it's a deal."

"No way."

"Adam has five cacadaemons," said the third boy.

"Cool."

Major Warthen looked sharply at Mother Grey at the sound of the name.

"Whoa, dude," the second boy said, turning the pages of one of the albums. "You have a flaming skull. What'll you take for it?"

"Nothing," the first boy said. "I want to keep it."

"So where do we meet now?" said the third boy. "Speaking of Adam."

"I don't want to meet at all," the second boy said.

"What are you, chicken?"

"Yeah. I'm chicken. I also want to keep my flaming skull where it is."

"What would be the point, anyway?" the first boy said. "What would we even get out of it now?"

Mother Grey tore her eyes from the display of video games, entertainments for children wherein they were encouraged to dismember little men and cause them to bleed in several colors, to meet the pointed stare of the sales clerk. "Help you with something?" he said. Strange; in this place she and the major were the ones who were weird.

"We're looking for Edward Warthen," she said. "Do you know whether he's been in here lately? A blond-haired boy, about so high . . ."

"You guys seen Eddie Warthen lately?" said the clerk to the three boys.

"Who?" said one.

"That kid Adam hangs with," another mumbled.

"Oh. Him. No, not in a couple of weeks."

"What about Adam?" said the major.

"Adam either," the first boy said. The others joined in: "Adam either." "No. We haven't seen 'em. Sorry."

"I wonder whether you could tell us Adam's last name," said Mother Grey.

"Adam's last name," the first boy repeated, and they all said, "No, sorry." "No, we don't know what his last name is. Do we?" "No."

"If you should happen to see either one of them, could you tell them to call Mother Grey?" she said. "Tell them it's okay, I think I can help them."

"Help them," said the boys. "Right. Okay. We'll tell them." "We'll be sure to tell them." "If we see them." "Right."

They left the shop with three pairs of brown eyes boring holes into their backs. "Do you think they know where Edward is?" said the major.

"They might," said Mother Grey. "If we're lucky, they'll tell him to get in touch." But something about the boys' demeanor told her not to expect a call anytime soon.

After she put the word out all over town for Adam and Edward to call her, Mother Grey left the major to the dubious comforts of his empty house and returned to the rectory at St. Bede's.

When she came in, she saw that the light on her answering machine was blinking. She pushed the play button and heard Father Bingley leaving a message to call him. Father Bingley? What in the world could he want? She called the number he had left, but the line was busy.

She went to the kitchen and fed the animals, her own Towser and Simon Ratcher's devilish cat, which she had named Scratch, because it was one of the devil's names and because he did. Scratch had decided to live in the kitchen on top of the refrigerator.

As she stirred some soup for herself, Mother Grey tried to imagine child-care inspector Mastrangelo's reaction to the sight of a snarling black cat on top of the refrigerator. *No animals in the food preparation areas, Mother Grey.* What was it actually going to cost her to start up this day-care center? Would she be forced to give up her pets? Although his leg was almost normal now, she still felt that Towser would have a hard time getting along without her. As for the cat, anyone in his right mind would take it straight to the pound. If she didn't give it a home, it was a doomed little beast.

The Lord will provide, she told herself. *Don't worry about the animals.*

At last she sat down on the flowered chair in front of the fire with Towser at her feet, a mug of soup in her hand, and Arthur Spelving's copy of *The Book of Ceremonial Magic* in her lap. Time to do battle with Satan. The first step was to study the enemy.

She read through the spells, searching for one

she thought she had seen that involved a severed head. In the course of her study she learned that when the spirits come around as a result of your magical efforts, you are supposed to say to them, "Litan, Izer, Osnas." At this they will bow down before you, the book said, "individually remarking, 'Nanther.' " *Nanther?*

Here was the peculiar spell Schwartz had told her about called the Hand of Glory. For a moment she tried to imagine the sort of person who would dismember old corpses for the purpose of summoning and controlling demons. She pictured such a one in a black hooded cape, skulking through the medieval night. Did he cut the corpse down first, or did he leave it hanging while he sawed away at the felon's lifeless wrist? Of course it had to be done after dark; anyone caught engaging in such activities in medieval times would have been burned for witchcraft. And then, having gone through all that unpleasantness to secure the required body part, then to try to extract grease . . .

She finished the soup and closed her eyes to rest them. It had been a long day.

The dream that she then had, snuggled under her warm afghan, was very real. There was a knock on her door, and she got up and looked out to see Dave Dogg standing on the doorstep. By his side was a huge brown corrugated box sealed with reinforced tape.

She opened the door and took him in her

arms, inhaling the particular smell of his clothes and skin. It was good to have him back.

"I couldn't stay away," he said.

"What's in the box?" she said.

"Something I got for you in Boston. I hope it's okay."

In her dream she struggled to get the tape off the end of the box and then finally ripped it open. An ocean of Styrofoam peanuts spilled out, revealing the scroll end of a violoncello.

She pulled the instrument all the way out of the box. Styrofoam peanuts clung to it, held by static electricity. It was not a Weaver. There were a few light scratches in the finish. A long crack in the back seemed to have been mended with some sort of space-age glue. But the smooth buttery touch of the varnished wood was like heaven, like being reunited with a loved person long dead. She plucked the strings. The tone was beautiful. She took the bow from the box and drew it gently across the strings. The vibration it made in her hands was like the purr of a cat coming home to its mistress.

Then she was awake, and the actual cat was in her lap on top of the book of spells, kneading the afghan and purring. She felt a terrible sadness. The Weaver was gone. She would never hold it again.

The cat continued to rub against her while she wept. Then the cuckoo clock struck eleven. She must have slept for a long time. She got up and blew her nose, chiding herself for a silly woman. It was time to go to bed.

14

"Two hundred thousand dollars," said Father Rupert Bingley. "It's an anonymous donation from someone interested in your work in the town."

Mother Grey's mind reeled. It had been surprising enough to find Bingley waiting in her office after morning Mass, but to hear him offering her huge sums of money was stupefying. At last. Enough money. But from whom? *Someone interested in my work?*

Who did she know with that much money? Rodman Sedgewick, of course, but he could hardly be said to be interested in her work. Furthermore he would give her almost anything other than something she could really use, least of all two hundred thousand dollars. But who? Well, no matter. Never question the Lord's will. She did it anyway: "Any strings attached to this?"

"Not really. Of course, it's to be spent on the day-care center, which has to be opened on schedule."

"Schedule calls for it to open a week from next Monday."

"A week from next Monday. Yes, I believe that was when you said you would have it open."

"That might not be possible, Father Bingley."

"Why not?"

Where to begin? She took out the file containing the list that the child-care facility inspectors had left with her.

"The inspectors were here from the state on Tuesday, and they found many things that will have to be taken care of before they allow us to open."

"Yes? And?"

"Even if we had unlimited funds, I'm not sure everything they want done could be done in a week and a half. You know how hard it is to get workmen. And with this weather—"

Bingley went, "Hem, hem," cracked his knuckles, and examined the front of his shirt. "The anonymous donor who gave us this money stipulated as a condition that the center was to open on time," he said.

"Why did he do that?"

"Why did he or she do that," said Bingley with a smirk. She noted that he was correcting her assumption without answering her question. It struck her that it was a question he had never asked himself, a question furthermore that he was not asking himself even now. Some people were so stupid that life could roll right past them without making the least impression. She tried again.

"Did you receive any indication from the anonymous donor that there might be some particular reason why the center had to open on schedule?"

Bingley examined his fingernails. "I'm not at liberty to say."

"Because one of the requirements of the state is a fire escape that goes all the way to the ground on the side of the building where we don't own the ground. I can buy it now, I guess, but you know how these real estate transactions go, Rupert. It could be a couple of months until the closing."

"Isn't it true, Mother Grey, that you're spending all of your time investigating some local murder case instead of tending to the legitimate needs of the community, such as St. Bede's child-care center?"

Mother Grey was speechless. For one thing, she had never before heard Bingley acknowledge that the community had any legitimate needs. Receiving no answer, he went on: "I'm sure if you apply your energies exclusively to this child-care center business, it will all go according to schedule, and you can put this gift to good use. You're not a detective, Mother Grey."

Many stinging remarks raced each other to

her lips, but the voice of wisdom said, *Be quiet.*
Agree with him. Take the money.

"You're so right, Father Bingley," she said.
"First things first. How much did you say the first
installment of this grant was?"

"Fifty thousand," he said. "Here's the check.
The rest will come later, provided you stick to
business and open on time." The check was drawn
on a bank account of the diocese. No clue there to
the identity of the anonymous donor.

"Thank you very much. Give my best to Mrs.
Bingley." She gave him a dazzling smile and
showed him to the door.

When she went back to the chancel after the
astonishing interview with Bingley, Mother Grey
noticed it again: a sour alcoholic smell in the
church. She had been dimly aware of it at morning Mass, but thinking nothing more than that
one of the communicants had been tippling the
night before, she dismissed it from her mind. Yet
it was still here, stronger than ever.

Her first thought was that a homeless person
or a backsliding member of St. Bede's AA group
had come inside to escape the weather. She
turned on all the lights and looked in every pew.
No one was there.

The smell seemed strongest in the chancel.
Could someone be sleeping it off in the organ
chamber? She took off the door and looked in.

The smell behind the organ was strong
enough to be quite unpleasant. The trapdoor leading downward was open. A patch of dim light

showed through. There was a draft blowing upward and out through it, carrying cold air and the bad smell.

Ducking her head to avoid the organ machinery, Mother Grey crept all the way in and took a good look through the trapdoor. Below the organ chamber was a small room whose single cobwebbed window let in enough gray light to show stone walls, an arched brick doorway, an earthen floor. Rats had been scratching around. There was a drop of blood on the earth, scuff marks, a trowel. Mother Grey had a very bad feeling.

She backed out and called Jack Kreevitch.

"There's something wrong under the organ," she told him.

"What do you mean?" he said.

"I think I've found the head."

Three uniformed Fishersville policemen came, Jack Kreevitch, Jimmy Finn, and the Nazi. "Slow crime day?" she said to them.

"We want to see this," said Jack. "Don't do anything yet. We're waiting for Cranmer."

Presently Detective Cranmer from the county arrived, bringing with him a number of technicians. It was very different from the burglary investigation that Jack Kreevitch and Jimmy Finn had conducted in the church. The stakes in a murder investigation were higher, and so the procedures were more painstaking, fingerprinting everything, photographing everything, collecting tiny samples of fibers and blood.

The trapdoor behind the organ was much

Kate Gallison

too small for a full-grown homicide detective to pass through, but there was another way into the room from the undercroft. She took them downstairs and let them in through the arched doorway, and then she went upstairs and sat on a choir bench with her back to the proceedings while Cranmer and one or more of his technicians did their work. She did not want to see them dig it up. This was one image she would sooner not retain for later.

They talked to each other and took pictures; the sound of voices and the glow of flashing lights traveled up through the trapdoor and out through the opening in the paneling. She would never again see the light from a flashbulb without thinking of bloody murder.

The tone of Cranmer's voice was very matter-of-fact. He did not scream "It's the head!" or "I found it!" or anything emotional like that. Still, it was evident from what she was able to overhear that the head was indeed buried in the earth under St. Bede's organ. The technicians disinterred the thing with the slow care of archaeologists.

While all this was going on, the uniformed police of Fishersville gathered around Mother Grey's choir bench, sometimes talking among themselves, sometimes reacting to the slowly unfolding events under the organ, sometimes standing in stony and uncomfortable silence. Mother Grey had one more question in her mind. "Tell me something, Jack," she said. "Is there a bowling alley in Frenchtown?"

"No," he said. "Why?"

"No reason."

"There's a roller rink, if you're looking for something to do," said Finn. "It's a nice rink."

"No, it's all right," she said. "I was just wondering where one could go bowling."

"No place," said Finn.

"Trenton," said Kreevitch. "You and Dave want to go bowling? Maybe Marla and I could come along, if we could get a sitter. She's been complaining that I never take her out."

"No, it's okay," she said. "It was just an idle question."

More silence, and then the announcement that the head had what appeared to be a bullet wound in it.

At this Kreevitch grew very uncomfortable. Mother Grey thought she heard him mutter a curse under his breath. "Looks almost like a wound from a three-fifty-seven hollow-point," someone behind the organ said.

Finn said, "Hey, Jack. Did Chief Harry tell you about the gun that kid brought in?"

"Yeah, he filled me in on that situation," said Kreevitch.

"I understand he was ticked."

"He wasn't too thrilled. Now I guess these guys from the county prosecutor's office need to know about it too. No prints on the damned gun, right?"

"No prints," said Finn. "Nothing you could use anyway." The Nazi cleared his throat but said nothing.

"It's probably time we started trying real hard to find Brother Rex," Kreevitch said.

"What about that John Doe they pulled off the ice floe?" the Nazi said.

"Who?"

"What, you didn't hear about that? I thought this was your case."

"That guy! I thought he was supposed to be some biker from across the river. Did you get a look at him?"

"Yeah, I saw him, but I don't know your friend Rex by sight."

"Did he look like a biker?"

"He looked like a loser. Drunk as a skunk. We figured he fell on the ice, hit his head, and broke his arm."

"Right, but what did he look like? I mean, a physical description."

"He looked mean, he looked greasy and hairy, he had Satan's face tattooed on his right hand. Not a good tattoo either. Height about five nine, weight a hundred sixty-five or so."

"I need to check this out," said Kreevitch. "You guys stick around here and tell me what happens."

They stuck around while Kreevitch slipped out the side door to the sacristy. Eventually the technicians got the head disinterred and took it away by the cellar stairs. Still Mother Grey sat quietly. She received the impression from things that were said that its aspect was unusually weird even for a severed head.

After the activity had mostly died down, Detective Cranmer came to her where she sat on the choir bench and told her about it. "It appears that the cause of death was a gunshot wound to the head," he said. "But there was something—maybe a symbol of some sort—drawn on the forehead. Does that mean anything to you? Maybe you don't want to hear about this. Should I talk to you later?"

"Beans," she said.

"Excuse me?"

She was beginning to remember the severed head spell. "You found black beans in the eyes, nose, mouth, and ears. Am I right?" she said.

"Yeah," he said. "How did you know?"

The John Doe who had been saved from the river was in 320B, the desk nurse told Kreevitch. "Christine is his nurse, if you want to talk about his case with anyone."

"Thanks." Kreevitch left the desk and proceeded down the pastel hallway, checking room numbers as he went.

The smell of hospital food hung in the air, boiled turnips or something. Some of the patients in the rooms he passed were sleeping, but most of them, old people for the most part, were propped up in bed having dinner. Three eighteen, three nineteen. Here it was.

A dark-haired man with a yellowish complexion was sitting up in a chair picking at his food. "Hi," said Kreevitch. "I'm looking for a John Doe."

"That's him over by the window," the man said. "He doesn't usually get visitors. You a relative?"

"Not that I know of," said Kreevitch. "I'm just here to see him."

The patient was Perskie, all right. He lay in the bed by the window with his head slightly elevated, a tube in his mouth and another in his left arm. The rails of the bed were up on either side. From slightly below the shoulder to the first joint of each of his fingers, his right arm was in a cast. His eyes were blackened. His face was pale. He was snoring.

"Hey, buddy," said Kreevitch. "Hey, Rex. Wake up." There was no response.

"They said he was twice drunk when they found him," said the other patient. "Twice drunk. Blood alcohol level point two two."

"Does he talk, ever?"

"He never wakes up. They say he's in a coma."

Kreevitch went over to him and patted him lightly on the cheek. "Rex," he said. "Hey, buddy. It's Jack." No reaction whatever.

"He probably hears you," said the other patient.

"How do you figure?"

"I read someplace that people in a coma can hear everything you say, they just can't respond to it. You have to be very careful what you say in front of them, because it all soaks right in."

"That would be a welcome change, in this

guy's case," said Kreevitch. "He never listens when he's awake."

"Still, if you say something in front of him, he can probably hear it."

An interesting idea. Kreevitch was suddenly overpowered by the temptation to communicate meaningfully with Rex. He bent down and put his lips to his ear.

"Yo, Rex," he said. "You sorry bastard. What did you want to shoot that guy for?"

Perskie stirred a little and moaned.

"It'll be a cold day in hell before I let you get your hands on your piece again, you asshole. And I'll tell you another thing. As soon as you wake up, I'm going to personally beat the living shit out of you. If I have to lose my badge anyway over this stupid mess, I might as well get some fun out of it."

The unconscious man stopped breathing for a full five seconds. Kreevitch, astounded, considered whether words could kill. Then with a ragged, gasping breath the patient resumed his rhythmic snoring.

Nurse Christine came in with a fresh bag of solution and began to hook it up to Perskie's intravenous unit. "Were you speaking to him?" she said. "What were you saying?"

"Nothing," said Kreevitch. "What's he got?"

"A severe brain concussion. He suffered a blow to the head, probably in a fall. Also the broken arm."

"Maybe we can do a paraffin test on his hand, find out whether he fired a gun recently."

"Which hand?" she said.

"I guess he's right-handed."

"Not for six weeks," she said. "Unless you can do it on his fingertips."

"I don't think so," said Kreevitch.

"What makes you think he fired a gun?"

"He's a murder suspect."

"Oh! You know who he is, then."

"Yeah. Name's Rex Perskie. So do you think he might be waking up anytime soon?"

"We can't tell. It might take an hour, or it might take a month. Head injuries like this aren't always predictable."

"Must have been some fall."

"We see a lot of victims of bad falls in this icy weather. Frankly it's surprising to me that he could have walked far enough to fall down, with the amount of alcohol he had in him."

"Yeah, well. I guess he was used to it," Kreevitch said. "Listen, I want you to call this number right away if he wakes up." He gave her Detective Cranmer's card. "Like I said, the man's a suspect in a murder case. We don't want him walking out of here."

"I don't think that will happen," she said. "Not anytime soon. But we'll be sure to call. By the way, could you stop by admissions on your way out and tell them who he is?"

"Glad to," he said.

After she went out again, he murmured in Perskie's ear one last time: "Die, you son of a bitch. Do us all a favor. Save the state a lot of money and trouble."

15

H ere it was.
  "*To Become Invisible.*

  "*Begin this operation on a Wednesday before the sun rises, being furnished with seven black beans. Take next the head of a dead man; place one of the beans in his mouth, two in his eyes and two in his ears. Then make upon this head the character of the figure which here follows.*"

There was no illustration in *Ceremonial Magic* for the figure that was supposed to be drawn on the head. Maybe the boys—she was almost certain now that the decapitation was the work of the boys—had made up a figure, or maybe the figure was included in the grimoire they were using. You definitely needed a figure, lest you be seized by a strange demon, as the rest of the spell made clear:

"This done, inter the head with the face towards heaven, and every day before sunrise, for the space of nine days, water it with excellent brandy. On the eighth day you will find the cited spirit, who will say unto you: What dost thou? *You shall reply:* I am watering my plant. *He will then say:* Give me that bottle; I will water it myself. *You will answer by refusing, and he will again ask you, but you will persist in declining, until he shall stretch forth his hand and show you the same figure which you have traced upon the head suspended from the tips of his fingers. In this case you may be assured that it is really the spirit of the head, because another might take you unawares, which would bring you evil, and further, your operation would be unfruitful. When you have given him your phial, he will water the head and depart.*

"On the morrow, which is the ninth day, you shall return and will find your beans ripe. Take them, place one in your mouth, and then look at yourself in a glass. If you cannot see yourself, it is good. Do the same with the rest, or they may be tested in the mouth of a child. All those which do not answer must be interred with the head."

"Well, I'll be damned," said Detective Cranmer. "'Scuse me, Reverend."

She tried to explain the implications. Nine days before the spell could work. Today was Friday. Whoever buried the head would be coming

---

back to sprinkle brandy on the thing every day for another week.

"I worked with a psychic once," Cranmer said.

"The point isn't that *I* believe in this spell," she said to him. "The point is that whoever did this believes in the spell. If they don't know that the head has been found, they're almost certain to come back here just before sunrise tomorrow morning."

It was conceivable that someone in Fishersville had missed seeing the crowd of law enforcement personnel converging on the church that morning, or had missed the ceremonial removal of the head. Not probable, perhaps, but conceivable. A glance out the front door of the rectory revealed a goodly number of Mother Grey's neighbors standing around in the snow gawking at the comings and goings. She drew her head inside and closed the door.

"You think they'll be back," said Cranmer.

He was starting to get it. "I think they'll be back," she said.

"Before sunrise tomorrow?"

"Sometime before sunrise. That's if they aren't aware yet that the head has been found." She herself was scarcely aware of it; the whole morning's activity seemed unreal. She thrust her hands into her pockets and began feeling the contents, trying to ground herself in physical reality.

"So they might come back. Wish you'd mentioned it earlier, before we parked all the cars out there," he said.

"I wasn't sure."

"What made you sure?"

"The beans."

"Right. Okay, then. We'll be here waiting for them."

She realized suddenly, speaking of unreality, that the piece of paper she had been feeling in her pocket was a check for fifty thousand dollars.

As soon as Detective Cranmer and the others were gone, Mother Grey set to work putting the money to good use, depositing it in the bank, calling workmen, stopping by the hardware store to pick up a few of the many things required by the state inspectors.

By the time she was able to get to the Warthens' house, the sun was going down again. No lights showed. It might be that the major was home just the same, sitting in the dark, or off in some part of the house that couldn't be seen from the front. She plied the knocker vigorously.

The door opened, and there stood the major, still in the dark. A miasma surrounded him, a physical thing that could only be described as an alcoholic fog.

"Vinnie," he said. He took her hand. His own was warm and moist in an unwholesome sort of way.

She pulled her hand away and went inside. "I'm here on a very serious matter, Armstrong. Have you heard from Edward yet?"

"Edward? No."

"I'm afraid he's in terrible trouble. He and his

241

friend Adam may be involved in the murder of Simon Ratcher."

"What makes you think so?"

What did make her think so? Maybe it wasn't them. But who else had a key to the church? Who else had been seen reading Satanist spell books? Who else dragged suspicious-looking bowling bags around and made up lies about nonexistent bowling alleys? "Strong evidence is pointing in their direction," she said.

"Doesn't matter," he said. "He's not here. He's gone. Everyone has gone away."

"Armstrong," she said to him, "I think you need help. All of you."

"I need you," he said. "You lovely woman." He made a dive toward her. Somehow he tripped over the coffee table and fell on his face on the soft pastel patterned rug.

"Armstrong?" she said. He gave a little smile and said, "Mmm," but he didn't open his eyes or get up. It appeared that he planned to remain there.

"My word," she murmured. "Stinko." She put a sofa pillow under his head and crept out.

She was actually able to sleep for several hours before everyone converged on St. Bede's for the long night's vigil. The official county and city police arrived shortly after midnight, very quietly, deploying their police vehicles some distance away, dispensing with lights and sirens.

The church was chilly. When no one was in it, the thermostat was kept at fifty-five degrees Fahrenheit to save fuel. Mother Grey and Detective Cranmer, conferring, decided that nothing should be changed in the usual nighttime routine. If Edward came in and found the radiators hissing, he might become suspicious and run.

So they sat in the chilly dark, waiting. A faint blue—you couldn't call it light, it was merely somewhat less dark—showed where the windows were, but nothing like light got inside. It was so dark that those who were waiting could not see one another. Mother Grey knew where the others were only by the sounds they made, muffled whispers and the occasional cough or clearing of a throat.

There were creaking sounds in the pews, too, not made by people, or at least not made by living people. Mother Grey knew those noises from her own times alone in the dark church on other nights. She never used to mind them at all but thought of them as familiar and friendly. But that was then. Now who could tell what spirits might get into her church, with children invoking demons of Satan in the organ chamber? Perhaps St. Bede's would have to be reconsecrated.

She had brought a thermos of black coffee, and from time to time she took a hot pungent swig. She wondered whether Edward might not open the door, get a whiff of coffee (or even the collective breath of the law enforcement officers waiting in the second row of pews), and bolt. But after a while the coffee was gone. Then the furnace started. They could hear its low roar and the hiss and clank of the radiators until the church warmed up again to 55. A scratching began, as of mice, and then subsided.

Hours went by. Eventually there was nothing to do in the silent church except pray.

A sudden puff of cold air told the watchers when the outside door of the sacristy was opened and then shut again. High whispering voices sounded. Sudden pale light flickered and then glowed, illuminating the octagonal blue-green stained-glass window between the sacristy and the chancel, casting a parallelogram of yellow light on the chancel's polished oak floor.

First one boy and then the other slipped into the chancel from the sacristy, each carrying an altar candle. Mother Grey almost expected to see them in long white nightgowns like Wee Willie Winkie, but what they were wearing was jeans and down coats. There was a smell of hot beeswax. *Here comes a candle to light you to bed, here comes a chopper to chop off your head.*

Struggling a little to hold his candle, Edward took down the door to the organ chamber and leaned it against the paneling. Adam, meanwhile, withdrew a flask from an inside pocket of his coat. His dark hair covered his face almost completely. Edward with his golden curls looked like a Renaissance angel; the candlelight shone through his slim fingers, making them appear red.

"Five more days," Adam said. "Then the spirit will come. Next day we can use the beans."

"Hey, give me that," Edward said.

"I want to do it this time," said Adam.

"You can't fit through the trapdoor, asshole. Give it here."

"Okay, here, then." The other boy passed him the flask. "I can't wait to see the demon with the sign," he said. "This will be truly cool."

First Edward and then Adam stepped into the organ chamber, candles in hand.

The police officers rose from their places in the pews and began to position themselves to make an arrest. One of them slipped softly out the door of the sacristy to cover the entrance to the little room from the undercroft. Two other officers crept to the opening in the organ paneling. Their silhouettes were just barely visible against the pre-dawn light. With horror Mother Grey saw them draw their weapons. *Surely that isn't necessary,* she thought, although it was true that Simon Ratcher had died of a gunshot wound. As far as the officers knew, the boys might easily be armed.

As soon as he was through the trapdoor and inside the little room, Edward perceived that their work had been disturbed. First he and then Adam began shouting; their cries of rage and disbelief echoed in the dark church. "What the—!" "Freak!" Edward's voice came from underneath the floor of the chancel, as from a tomb.

It was Mother Grey who turned on the lights.

She heard the voices of the police officers telling the children to keep their hands in sight, and then they appeared, handcuffed, Adam from under the organ chamber and Edward from the doorway to the chancel, where an officer had brought him up from the undercroft and in through the outside door. Once apprehended, the boys put up no resistance but stood in bewilderment as the county detective read them their rights. All they seemed to comprehend was that their experiment was ruined.

"Couldn't you just—couldn't you just bury it again, like right now, and put the brandy on it before the sun comes up?" Edward pleaded. "Maybe the spirit won't notice you messed with it."

"What did you guys think was going to happen?" Cranmer asked him.

"We were going to get invisible," Adam said. "It was all in this book. Simon translated these spells for us and then he said we should try one of them."

"But it's hard to find most of the stuff you need," said Edward. "Baby goats. They don't have them in Fishersville."

"So you cut off Simon Ratcher's head."

"Adam told me to do it," Edward said. "Actually he was just kidding, but I thought he meant for me to do it, so I did it."

"Simon would have wanted us to," said Adam. Breathtaking. "You thought Simon Ratcher wanted you to cut off his head?" said Mother Grey. The irony of it. With his stupid black magic, Ratcher had created the monster that destroyed him. But wait. Ratcher didn't die of decapitation.

"He was dead already," said Adam. "He didn't

need his head. We needed it. He would have wanted us to take it to work the spell."

"Dead men's heads aren't all that easy to find, in case you haven't noticed," Edward said.

"So you found his body, and you—"

"Adam said, 'He's dead. Let's get his head for the invisibility spell.'"

"I was kidding," said Adam.

"But I thought he was serious. So there was this ax right there, and I just . . ."

"He did it," Adam said. "I never really told him to."

"Then we had to find someplace to bury it. Only since the ground was all frozen, we couldn't just bury it in the yard," Edward said.

"Eddie remembered the room under the organ," said Adam.

Cranmer said, "What were you boys going to do after you became invisible?"

"I don't know. It would just be cool," said Edward.

"Cool," Mother Grey repeated. She wanted to scream at the boy. His scientific curiosity—was that what it was?—had destroyed his life. And he still didn't understand this. All he understood was that now that the two of them had been caught, he would never know whether the demon would come, or whether magic beans could make you invisible.

What else had they done? "Did you kill the cats?" she asked him.

"The other kids did it," Edward said.

247

"Because there weren't any goats," Adam explained.

"And I let them keep them in my freezer," Edward said. "We were going to use them to make spell parchment, but then Uncle Rodman came and took them all away."

Edward, looking from one grim grown-up face to another, was beginning to realize how much trouble he was in. He asked to go to the bathroom and said that he had to throw up.

The eastern sky was streaked with peach by the time Detective Cranmer's unmarked car pulled away from the church to take the two suspects to the youth house. It was time for a very unpleasant interview with Major Armstrong Warthen, conducted by phone this time; since Edward and Adam were in custody, they wouldn't be tying it up communing with the Satanism bulletin board. She went back to the rectory and called the Warthens' number while the coffee dripped. Coffee. It smelled wonderful. There was something to be said about the good old cowboy values.

After three rings, an unexpected voice answered, that of Rodman Sedgewick.

"Is Major Warthen there?"

"I'm afraid he's unavailable right now, Miss . . ."

"It's Mother Grey. I understand that he's having problems, Rodman, but I need to talk to him."

"The major isn't here," said Sedgewick. "He's on his way to the Lavenhill Clinic. He's quite ill.

Is it important? I can give him a message when he . . . recovers."

Important? Why no. I always get my parishioners out of bed at six in the morning for trivialities. "I'm calling about Edward," she said. "He's been arrested."

"Has he."

"He's confessed to cutting off Simon Ratcher's head. Have you any idea how I can get in touch with Ellen?"

"No," he said. "No idea."

16

The phone woke her. The clock told her it was five of eleven. She had to think to remember it was Saturday.

"Hi, it's Saraleigh."

"Good morning, dear. What's up?"

"Good news and bad news."

Mother Grey sighed. She hated games, especially when she had just wakened from a sound sleep. Nevertheless, she played along: "What's the good news?"

"They let Ralphie out. He came home a few minutes ago. We can have the wedding this afternoon. If you still want to marry us."

"Have you got the license?" City Hall would be closed until Monday.

"Yeah. That's all okay."

"Well, certainly. You can be married right on schedule, the way we planned. What's the bad news?"

"Freddy is in the youth house."

Freddy? "Whatever for?"

"Now they're saying *he* shot that antique dealer." The county prosecutor's office had decided that since the whole thing was the work of a kid gang, any kid they found was probably part of it. Tests had proved that neither Edward nor Adam had fired a gun anytime in the recent past, so they had taken Freddy in to do the test on him.

Mother Grey still didn't understand. "But why Freddy?"

"He turned in the gun."

"What gun?"

"The gun that killed the antique dealer."

Clearly there was some mistake. Mother Grey told Saraleigh not to worry, and then she hung up and pulled her hair.

She called Martine to plan their next legal move. "Saraleigh and Ralph are all set to go ahead with the wedding at three o'clock," she said to Martine, "but it will be a shame if Fred can't come to see them get married."

"We'll get him there," said Martine. "I'll get over to the youth house right now and try to get him out."

"Can you do that?"

"I think I can. It depends on whether they did this paraffin test yet, or what the outcome was."

"I hope Ralph finds his job waiting for him at

the paper-bag factory," Mother Grey said. "I don't know what Saraleigh will do for medical coverage for those children if he loses his insurance. I just hope nobody gets hurt or sick."

"No problem," Martine said. "Saraleigh won't lose her benefits by marrying. Under New Jersey law, all her children would continue to be covered by Medicaid."

"Really?"

"They changed that law years ago. I can't believe no one in the welfare office told her."

"Could she have forgotten?"

"She could have forgotten," said Martine. "Or she could have decided to wait and see whether Ralph could hold a job before she married him."

"In a rare burst of good sense," said Mother Grey.

"Really," said Martine. "But you know, Mother Vinnie, Saraleigh isn't as dumb as people think."

"The wedding is at three," said Mother Grey.

"Right," said Martine. "I'll go to the youth house and see whether I can get them to release Freddy."

So now there was almost nothing for Mother Grey to do but go forward with the joyous preparations. She called Delight van Buskirk about the cake, only to discover that the old lady in her hillside farmhouse had heard nothing of Ralph's legal difficulties and had gone ahead and baked it. She was putting the icing on even then. "There'll be bride's cake on the top," said Mrs. van Buskirk. "It's like fruitcake. It keeps. You can sleep with a piece of it under your pillow and dream of the man you'll marry."

"I can hardly wait," said Mother Grey.

"So that strange man is dead," she said. "Do you have any idea yet who it was that killed him?"

"Not really."

"You're sure it wasn't Ralph."

"I'm quite certain."

"Because if you think you can make a good guess, Mother Vinnie, you better tell somebody before you walk down any dark alleys."

"I will, Mrs. van Buskirk," she said. "Trust me."

Now there was just one other pastoral duty for Mother Grey to do, rather a tricky one. As she pulled off the highway onto the narrow secondary road, she considered the life and character of Simon Ratcher. Suddenly she understood who had shot the antique dealer and why. She was unable to keep her promise to Mrs. van Buskirk, since there was no telephone in the car, but she couldn't imagine that it really mattered. *I can't believe this could actually be dangerous*, she said to herself.

Rodman Sedgewick's establishment in the country was not visible from the road. A small sign proclaiming BOUNTIFUL HORSE FARMS with a picture of a horse in an English saddle was all you could see of it, even with the leaves off the trees. It would have been easy to miss it altogether.

Well plowed, strewn with ashes, the driveway wound up and over a hill. From the top of the hill,

Mother Grey could take in the true scope of the property, the house, the pool, the outbuildings, the racetrack, and then the fields, Sedgewick land as far as the eye could see. She pulled the Nova onto a flat place in the shadow of the hedgerow at the top of the hill. Once started down the steep grade to the parking area beside Sedgewick's house, there was no telling whether the car would make it back up, with its valves in their present shape.

As she started down the driveway on foot (luckily her shoes were flat and waterproof), none other than Rodman Sedgewick himself rode up on horseback and greeted her. The view of him that met her eye, being at eye level, was of a well-muscled calf in a polished brown boot.

Funny, I never noticed his legs before. "I need to talk to Ellen. She's here, isn't she?" Mother Grey said.

He gave her a hard stare but did not deny this time that his sister was on the premises. "You'll find her in the horse barn," he said, pointing toward it with a gesture of his riding crop. "Look in the tack room." He turned the horse and trotted away.

Rodman Sedgewick's horse barn was not far from the house, over a little rise and down a hill. It looked small at first until Mother Grey saw that the barn was built into the side of the hill, so that the barn door that faced the house gave onto a second story. In order to get to where the horses were, one had to walk around to the lower side of the barn.

There was a small door about halfway down the north side of the barn. It wasn't locked. Mother Grey pushed it open and stepped into the huge black steamy space.

"Ellen?" she called into the darkness. A horse whinnied.

Mother Grey was nervous around large animals. Even as a girl, she had never been a horse person. Hiking the mountains was her sport, the clean fresh air, the hope of never meeting livestock. One of the horses stamped its feet, a heavy menacing sound. Best take a deep breath and march right in. Anyway, they didn't keep the horses in the tack room, did they? "Ellen?"

No answer. It was necessary to walk past a number of large horses hulking in their stalls to reach the faintly lighted rectangle that seemed to be the entrance to the tack room. As she groped her way along, something furry touched her leg. She started and looked down to see the gleaming green eyes of the barn cat. It meowed.

"Kitty!" she said softly. "How's the kitty?" She picked it up and petted it a little, then put it down. It ran into the tack room.

Mother Grey followed the cat and found herself at one end of a long room, low-ceilinged, running almost the length of the barn. There were smells of saddle soap, coal smoke, and horse. A coal fire glowed in the belly of a small stove. Through the snow-covered windows came enough light to see the long wall where polo mallets, helmets, saddles, and other sorts of tack were stored on shelves and hooks, to see the well-used work counter, nicked and stained, where brushes, paints, and water were set out, to see Ellen Warthen at her easel. She was working on a view of the room, nicely done, capturing accurately the brown glow, the glints of brass. The picture was almost finished.

"Very nice," Mother Grey said, looking over her shoulder.

"Vinnie! So you came looking for me."

"I've been looking for you all week. We all have. I wonder why Ouida didn't tell me you were here when I spoke to her."

"Ouida doesn't know I'm here. She never comes out here. Actually, my sister-in-law doesn't like horses."

"Why did you come here?"

"I had to get away to try to think," she said. "Can you understand?"

"I believe so."

"You know I grew up here. This place relaxes me. I would have come back eventually. How is Edward?"

"He's in very serious trouble, Ellen. That's why I've come. He's been arrested in connection with Simon Ratcher's murder."

"Edward? Why?"

"He and another boy cut off Ratcher's head." Mother Grey blurted it out, not being able to think of any way to soften the news. The brush, still wet with dark paint, fell from Ellen's hand.

"Oh, my God. Was he . . . was he trying to protect me somehow?"

"No, I'm afraid it was some stupid stunt to make themselves invisible. He never knew you were the one who killed Simon Ratcher."

"I'll have to go back right away then." She put the tubes of paint back in the box, carefully, making sure each tube went into the right groove.

"I think you should," said Mother Grey.

"I never meant to shoot him," she said. "I went to the Umbrella Works to talk to him. Edward had said some things about what they did over there."

"Sexual abuse."

"Armstrong wouldn't pay any attention, but I was so worried. I almost talked to you about it. It was the night I called and you came over. I wish now that I had spoken to you."

"So you went to talk to Simon Ratcher the next day, to find out whether the things Edward accused him of were true," Mother Grey said.

"Did you know that Simon had offered to handle my work? He had a friend who ran a gallery in New York." There was an edge of bitterness to her voice. So that was what was between them: the lure of artistic fulfillment, of self-actualization. Perhaps it was for this reason that Ellen had not seen Simon Ratcher as he appeared to Mother Grey, a slimy seducer. Yes, the wretched fellow had tried to seduce even Mother Grey herself, to lure her into selling off the property of the church for money. He had tempted her. Money. You could do so much good with the stuff, if only you could get your hands on it.

Ellen continued her story. "I came through the bushes from our house, which as you know is just half a block away from the factory. Suddenly a gun seemed to come from nowhere and fell right at my feet. I picked it up the way anybody would. I thought it was strange, but I didn't see anyone around and so I went inside to find Simon and talk to him. I walked into the shop. He was standing behind one of his display cases, and there on top of the case I saw a photograph." She started to cry. "My poor little boy," she said. "My baby."

"So you shot him because of what you saw in the photograph."

"Simon taunted me. He seemed to think that because he was promoting my art career, he was somehow entitled to Edward. He said I knew all along what was going on, that I was a hypocrite. Could he be right? Did I know? How could I have known?"

"What a horrible man," said Mother Grey.

"Suddenly I saw red. I'd never felt like that before. If I hadn't had the gun in my pocket, I would have used something else, just picked up anything and beaten him with it, one of his sculptures or whatever. Did Edward really cut off his head?"

"It seems so."

"This is Armstrong's fault," she said, running a hand through her hair. "I never should have married him. You know, I think all he wanted me for was my money. He never really—and he was so stiff with the children. If I'd known how things would turn out—"

"We can't predict everything," said Mother Grey. "Sometimes you just do the best you can and leave it in God's hands." She heard herself mouthing these platitudes and was mildly revolted. *How inadequate I feel to this calling sometimes.* What do you say to comfort a murderer? They hadn't taught her that in seminary, and it didn't come naturally.

"Celia is pregnant, you know," Ellen said. "That was Armstrong's fault too." Mother Grey braced herself for revelations of incest, but Ellen continued, "He was so strict with Celia when she was growing up that naturally she got pregnant her first year in college."

"I suppose he was strict with Edward too."

"Very strict. So poor Edward got involved with the first child molester who came along." She produced the picture. "I was going to destroy this, but then I thought it might be needed for something."

It was like the others, the ones that were still in Mother Grey's bottom drawer in a manila envelope addressed to Simon Ratcher. Except that this one had Edward in it, with Adam. "I think you'll definitely need this when your case comes to trial," Mother Grey said. "It will be important for your defense. Have you talked to a lawyer yet?"

"No."

"Do you want me to call Martine?"

Ellen smiled, a touch patronizingly, and said, "Dexter and Weatherby usually handle my legal affairs. I'll give them a call before I come with you."

They heard one of the horses nicker and stamp, and Rodman Sedgewick appeared in the doorway. "Good morning, ladies."

"Hello, Roddy," said Ellen.

"Does he know?" Mother Grey asked her. *Well of course he knows,* she told herself. Didn't he get Rupert Bingley to offer her two hundred thousand dollars to direct her attention away from the case? And why? To protect his sister? Maybe. But more likely to protect his political career.

"Roddy has been very good," Ellen said. "Let me wash my brushes and call Frank Weatherby. Then I'll let you drive me to the police station, if you'll be kind enough, Mother Vinnie."

"I can't believe you're going to cave in to this woman, Ellen," said Rodman Sedgewick.

"What do you mean?" she said.

"She has no proof against you."

"Roddy, I just told her everything."

"Deny it. It's your word against hers."

"Roddy, Edward has been arrested. He needs my help."

Sedgewick said, "Edward is perfectly safe. He was released from the youth house and is now in Lavenhill Clinic under heavy sedation. Dr. Gelb is taking care of him. There's nothing you can do for him by turning yourself in. It will only cause a lot of publicity."

"Is that your solution to everything, Rodman?" said Mother Grey. "Put all the problem people away in the Lavenhill Clinic? Hush it all up?"

"It works as well as anything else," he replied. "Be fair, Mother Grey. Edward is a very troubled boy. Wouldn't you say he belonged there?"

"And what about young Adam?"

"Adam Reeker?" *Ah. A last name, finally.* "Nothing of him. He isn't important. A little punk."

The Reekers, Mother Grey reflected, were among the founding families of Fishersville. It was true that the last two or three generations of Reekers seemed to have gone to the bad. Adam's grandfather, for instance, was the town drunk. But unimportant? How dare he? "The Reekers were honest farmers tilling the soil of Fishersville when your people were trading rum for slaves," Mother Grey said. It was a shot in the dark. She actually knew nothing about the foundation of the Sedgewick family fortunes.

Sedgewick ignored the insult. "Why did you have to concern yourself with this business at all? Why couldn't you have just shut up and let Ralph Voercker take the rap? What good is a person like Voercker? Or Fred Kane. My nephew has much more of a future than that little bastard."

"Surely the legitimacy of his parenthood isn't the issue, Rodman," Mother Grey said. "The child is innocent of wrongdoing."

"I'll be blunt, then," said Sedgewick. "Go home

261

and leave this alone, or you'll never see another cent from me for your day-care center."

Mother Grey tossed her head. "St. Bede's doesn't need your money. I can write a grant proposal," she said. "There are more funds available out there than you think." So the day-care center wouldn't be open next week. Nobody really expected it to open next week anyhow. These things took time. "Let's go, Ellen."

Ellen was standing motionless, her brushes drying in her hand. Was she trying to make up her mind? "Come on," Mother Grey said to her. Her only response was to look down at the brushes, a frown puckering her forehead.

"Come on," she said again. "Innocent people will suffer if you don't come forward. I know you don't want that."

"All right," she said. She put the brushes down unwashed and picked up a woolen scarf to wrap her head with. "Just let me call Frank Weatherby first."

Sedgewick looked from one to the other of them, a queer sort of speculation in his eye. Mother Grey didn't like it. She had seen that look before. He picked up a polo mallet and hefted it in his hand.

"Call him from the police station," said Mother Grey. "Or I can call him for you." She took her by the coat sleeve and gave a tug.

Sedgewick put himself between them and the door. "I'm sick of you women," he said. "I mean to go to Washington next year, and I'm not going to let either of you stand in my way. Nobody knows where you are, Mother Grey. You won't be missed. Nor you, Ellen, as long as you seem to want to persist in this."

He meant to kill her. *I can't possibly die right now. I have a wedding to perform this afternoon,* she told herself. She glanced around, looking for a means of defense. Maybe she could keep him talking.

"I think I should tell you, Rodman, that the last person who threatened my life is dead." To say this gave her a queer feeling of pride, and she realized that in some corner of her flawed character, she enjoyed triumphing over her enemies. She would enjoy getting the better of Rodman Sedgewick, if things worked out that way.

Which was beginning to look doubtful. Sedgewick took a two-handed swing at her head. She ducked. The blow struck Ellen on the shoulder, knocking her to the floor. Mother Grey retreated a step and put the easel between them. He came on.

She pushed the easel over onto him. He dodged and stumbled. As he recovered his balance, she retreated again. "Ellen, run!" she cried.

Ellen sat there like a sack of gelatin. "Why? Why should I run?" she said. "Do you think I have a life left anywhere?"

17

Even as he made his pastoral rounds to bring the Eucharist to the aged and infirm at the Sunset Acres Nursing Facility, Father Rupert Bingley chewed over his latest humiliation at the hands of Mother Lavinia Grey.

Money for outreach. It could have been his. But Mother Grey had started a project while Bingley was still dithering over the appearance of his church. Now Bingley's richest and most powerful parishioner was bankrolling that woman, that impostor priest. (Women priests! Bah!) Bingley felt suddenly that his entire ministry was obsolete, left in the dust along with the 1928 prayer book. He gazed into the clouded blue eyes of old Mrs. Soames. He squeezed her withered hand and murmured a word of encouragement. All the while he was thinking, *Before very long I'll be right here with the rest of you vegetables, old and useless. Who will remember me? What will I have accomplished?*

"How are we feeling today, Mrs. Wertz?" he asked his next communicant. Mrs. Wertz had been a vigorous woman before her stroke; Bingley remembered with what energy she had spearheaded the painting of the interior of St. Dinarius in the days before they could afford professional painters. Even now she seemed mentally sharp and energetic, though she was confined to a wheelchair.

"I'd feel better if Serena were here," the old lady said.

"Serena?"

"The nurse who takes care of us. Lovely girl. Haven't seen her in a week."

"Indeed."

"Her baby-sitter has the flu, so she can't get out of the house. She has to stay home with the little ones."

"Too bad."

"The home is short-handed without her, too, and everyone is cross. You'd think there would be some reliable place a mother could leave her children for a few hours."

"Wouldn't you think so, Mrs. Wertz."

Father Bingley went on about his ministrations, but old Mrs. Wertz's words lodged deep in his mind. On the road home to Rolling Hills, they sprouted like the mustard seed in Our Lord's par-

able, and suddenly bore forth a rich crop of . . .
well, mustard.

The Rupert L. Bingley Child Care Center.

Or even the Rodman Sedgewick Child Care
Center. Father Bingley was not a vain man. Knowing that the idea was his own, that he had caused
it to come into being, would be reward enough. A
place where children of all faiths and races could
blossom. A place where his own grandchildren
would not be unhappy to play and grow. A nur-
turing place.

Just as this vision appeared to him, Father
Bingley noticed the sign for Bountiful Horse
Farms by the side of the road. A glance up the
driveway revealed a gray Chevy Nova parked under the shadow of the hedgerow.

Mother Grey. Here. So the grant of money
hadn't been enough for her. She must have found
out where it came from. She must have come here
to lure his richest and most influential parishioners away from St. Dinarius.

But what was she using as bait to get the
Sedgewicks to attend St. Bede's? The charm of her
nineteenth-century church? They had never cared
about such things in the past. Her skill as a
preacher? Bingley had never heard that she had
any great aptitude in that area. The neediness of
the place? That must be it. Rodman Sedgewick in
his public-spirited generosity was undoubtedly
considering defecting to St. Bede's because he
imagined St. Bede's needed him. (Actually what

St. Bede's needed was to be torn down in a timely manner. But that campaign was for another day.)

Right now it was time to do battle for the Sedgewicks. He would redirect their generosity toward something more appropriate, something with a chance of success, something sponsored by himself and St. Dinarius, which was after all the Sedgewicks' parish church. He must sell them his own vision of a day-care center.

There was no time like the present. He turned into the well-salted drive and proceeded to the house. He would share with them his dream, the great work to which he could put the Sedgewicks' money and still keep them in the fold. Ouida's car was parked next to the house; she must be home. He would pretend to make a pastoral call and casually mention his project.

Ouida answered the door. "Father Bingley! How nice to see you! And what a surprise."

"Nice to see you too. Actually I've come to see Rodman." He glanced over her shoulder and saw that the living room was empty. No poaching priestesses from neighboring parishes here. Where was Mother Grey?

"Roddy is out riding, Father Bingley. He should be back in a little while. Would you like some tea?"

"Riding? Then where is Mother Grey?"

"Mother Grey? Should she be here?"

"Her car is in your driveway," said Bingley. "I think it's hers. Perhaps I was mistaken."

Ouida Sedgewick looked suddenly and inexplicably grim. "Perhaps they're in the horse barn," she said through gritted teeth. "We'll . . . just . . . see." She slipped on a coat and headed out the door. Father Bingley trailed along behind her, bewildered. What would Mother Grey and Rodman Sedgewick be doing in the horse barn?

Not what Ouida Sedgewick was thinking.

Mother Grey, backed into a corner, prepared to fend off Rodman Sedgewick's latest assault. She cast a frantic look around the tack room for a fresh means of defending herself. So far in their struggles, sawhorses, chairs, saddles, and assorted tack had been knocked to the floor. As Ellen Warthen crouched by the doorway in near-catatonic paralysis, Sedgewick, snarling, sweating, redfaced, came at Mother Grey with the polo mallet.

Talk was useless. In vain Mother Grey reminded him of his duty as a Christian, in vain pointed out that clubbing a clergywoman to death would surely mean the end of his political career.

"Shut up!" he said. "Just shut up!" and swung at her again.

Again he missed by inches. She put her hand out to steady herself and clutched what proved to be another polo mallet.

Clearly it was from God, a gift of self-defense. Martial arts training would have made it somewhat more useful; Sedgewick was twice her size and very fit. Still, Mother Grey was resolved to do her duty. *Here goes*, she thought. Sedgewick struck again, and this time she was able to parry the stroke and land one of her own, a solid blow to the right kneecap that caused him to roar.

While he was bending over feeling his knee, she threw a handful of bran in his eyes and gave him a good clip on the ear. The fight got pretty hot then. It was graceless and ugly, not like Errol Flynn and Basil Rathbone. Her strategy was to hit him, hit him as often as she could land a blow, taking advantage of her size and quickness. Sedgewick fended her off as best he could, but he was not expecting this ferocity. At last he tripped and fell over the tack. He was wide open.

I can get him now. I can knock the top of his head right off. Seeing in her mind's eye the man's brains dashed all over the tack room, she suddenly realized how angry she was at Dave Dogg. It took her breath away. She dropped the mallet.

Sedgewick got to his feet and came after her one more time.

But just as he drew back his polo mallet to take a final swing, the barn door creaked, voices murmured, and the horses nickered and stamped. Ouida Sedgewick appeared in the doorway, wide-eyed, clutching the front of her camel-hair coat to her neck. Behind her stood Father Rupert Bingley, of all people, holding his homburg against his stomach, his bald head gleaming pink.

"Roddy!" said Ouida. "What are you doing?" Sedgewick lowered his arm and turned to face her.

"I noticed your car, Mother Grey," said Bingley. "We thought—" He caught sight of Ellen Warthen sitting on the floor nursing her shoulder and fell silent.

Ouida Sedgewick laughed. "You people wouldn't believe what this looks like," she said. "Ellen, why didn't you tell me you were here?"

"I—"

Mother Grey recovered her composure. "Ellen is with me," she said. "We were just leaving." Sedgewick dropped the hand holding the polo mallet and drew the back of the other across his forehead. He appeared to be more shocked and upset than Mother Grey herself about what he had almost done. She thought of Deedee and her theory about Anglo-Saxon men being out of touch with their feelings. *I had no idea I was capable of murder, Your Honor, until suddenly . . .*

And not only the men. *My word, I could have killed him.*

Father Bingley didn't seem to notice anything amiss. "I'm glad to find you at home, Rodman," he said. "I've had the most wonderful idea for a day-care facility for the children of the county. I'd like to discuss it with you. With the existing facilities we have in place at St. Dinarius, we would have only to hire staff and purchase a small amount of equipment. We could easily take care of forty children, and with the right kind of backing we could open a week from Monday—"

"Are you all right, Roddy?" said Ouida. "What were you all doing out here?"

"Rodman was showing us one of his polo

moves," said Mother Grey. "But we really must leave. It's good to see you, Father Bingley." The old blister seemed to have saved their lives, actually.

"Yes, it's—it's nice to run into you, Mother Grey."

"What's this about a child-care center?" she said.

"A new project of mine," said Bingley, fingering his hatbrim. "Since you were having such difficulties in Fishersville with inadequate facilities, I thought—"

"You thought to take up the slack at St. Dinarius," she said.

"Why, yes. As you know, our parish hall is quite extensive and all on the ground floor. We have no problem with fire exits."

Was that why he was here? Had Bingley come to this wretched horse barn to enlist the aid of Rodman Sedgewick in stealing St. Bede's day-care center away from her?

Mother Grey's first impulse was to pick the polo mallet up again and take a swing at Bingley's hairless pink pate. Was there no limit? Was there nothing the man wouldn't stoop to in his efforts to aggrandize St. Dinarius's at the expense of St. Bede's? But even as the blood of rage mounted to her cheeks, a voice, perhaps the voice of the Holy Spirit itself, whispered in her ear: *Let Bingley have the day-care center.*

Suddenly it made sense. St. Dinarius's parish hall had a number of large rooms, all on one floor, as Father Bingley had pointed out. They were used for Sunday school; they would be perfectly suitable for day care. Ideal, even. Several bathrooms, a lovely big kitchen for fixing lunches, no animals in residence that she knew of. Let Bingley have the day-care center. Let him deal with Childcare Facility Inspector Mastrangelo and his handmaidens. Let him deal with Rodman Sedgewick's so-called gifts, his threats, his temper. Let him fend off Sedgewick's attempts to use his money to bully and control. Actually Sedgewick's threats would be wasted on Bingley, who was too thick to understand what was required of him. It was made in heaven.

"What a coincidence!" said Mother Grey. "Rodman was just telling us how dear the subject of child care was to his heart. Wasn't he, Ellen? Get up, dear." She took Ellen by her good arm and pulled her to her feet. "He was saying how important it was, and what a shame it was that there weren't more chances to invest in it."

"What?" said Sedgewick. Ouida glanced from one to the other of them, trying to follow the conversation. She was still smiling, but the smile might have been a little forced.

Mother Grey reached into the inner pocket of her jacket where the résumés were, the ones she was going to evaluate as soon as she got a minute. "Here," she said, thrusting them into Father Bingley's hand. "You'll need professional staff, of course. There are undoubtedly some excellent candidates here. With Rodman's help, you'll be able to pay them what they're worth."

Bingley pocketed the résumés and shook her hand. His face was effulgent, an almost fanatical gleam in his eye. "Thank you, thank you, Mother Grey," he said. "You have no idea what this means to me." Truly God's grace was astonishing and came when you least expected it. Father Bingley had suddenly abandoned himself in his declining years to the joy of good works.

Rodman Sedgewick stood reeling, having been overtaken by the speed of events. The polo mallet fell from his fingers. As Father Bingley advanced on him, happily describing his plans for the two hundred thousand dollars, Mother Grey pulled Ellen toward the door. They left the watercolor paints and easel behind and made swift tracks through the stalls of horses.

As they came out of the steamy barn into the cold crisp morning, Ellen began to cry. "Does your shoulder hurt very much?" Mother Grey asked her.

"No, it isn't that," she said. "I'm just so sorry." All the way back up the driveway to Mother Grey's car, she said, "I'm sorry, Vinnie, I'm sorry," over and over again. She was so unstrung that Mother Grey was tempted to take her to the Lavenhill Clinic instead of to county police headquarters. But there would be time for that later. Her lawyers could take care of it, her lawyers and her brother.

* * *

The road back to Fishersville, salted and sun-lit, carried Mother Grey to the church in plenty of time to prepare St. Bede's for the Kane-Voercker wedding. The church was glorious. Rays of winter sun slanted through the stained-glass windows. Some miracle had preserved the white flowers from the wedding of the week before, or more than half of them at least; she took a turn around with a pair of scissors and snipped off the wilted ones.

Just before the wedding party arrived at St. Bede's, the pickup truck came around from Bountiful Horse Farms and backed onto the rectory lawn, soft and muddy now that the snow and ice had melted. When she went outside to see what was up, Mother Grey found Rodman Sedgewick's sons loading the freezer back in.

"What are you doing?" she said.

"Dad said since Father Bingley was doing the day-care center, he should have the freezer," said Chip.

"He said to remind you about the fifty thousand dollars," said Lance. "He said you have to give that back too."

"But—" Before she could explain or protest, they slammed the doors to the truck and drove away, gunning the engine, digging twin trenches in her poor unhappy lawn. "I hope you like the dead cats," she murmured.

* * *

274

Everyone declared that there had never been such an excellent day for a wedding.

Ralph came to his wedding dressed in a suit. Where he had acquired it, Mother Grey wasn't certain—perhaps the thrift basement at St. Joseph the Worker. The cut seemed a few years out of fashion. The suit fit him, though. He seemed to have lost a few pounds while he was in jail, and his new weight looked good on him.

Saraleigh was radiant. Dressed all in white, she was still somewhat bizarre in her habiliments (Mother Grey could see both tattoos from where she stood, or at least the two she knew of) but radiant. You know how it is with brides. Danny Handleman from the group home served as best man, Martine Wellworth was matron of honor, and Freddy Kane was there to bear the ring, wearing his little suit and tie and hating it.

Every friend the couple had in town was there, and that came to quite a few people. The church was almost full. From time to time as she read the service, Mother Grey glanced past Ralph's shoulder to be sure no disruptive influences were invading her church. She wasn't sure who it was she was expecting; demons saying "Nanther," perhaps, or policemen coming to arrest Ralph again, or maybe even Rex Perskie himself. But when she invited the congregation to show just cause why they might not lawfully be married, nobody said anything at all.

At that moment in the county medical center, the man in bed 320B stirred and opened his eyes.

"Saraleigh! Where is that bitch?" he mumbled. He drew a hand across his forehead, examined the needle protruding from his left wrist, felt the hard plaster of the cast on his other arm. Suddenly he sat straight up in bed and bellowed, so loudly that metal objects three rooms away vibrated harmonically, and all the sleeping patients awoke from their naps: "Saraleigh! I want my *woman*!" And then, "Where the hell are my *pants*!" But the sound of his cries did not carry to Fishersville. Ralph and Saraleigh were man and wife.

In a deep window embrasure in the chancel, Mother Grey kept the old brass alms basin, a treasure of St. Bede's that had been given to the church a hundred years before in memory of Mary Withers Wagonner. Being in the embrasure, it was partly hidden from view, and so the burglar had passed it by. When the wedding was over, Mother Grey suddenly noticed that the alms basin held an envelope. She thought it curious. They hadn't taken up a collection.

In the envelope she found ten thousand dollars in wrinkled hundreds and twenties.

My word.

Clearly this was some anonymous gift from someone who had come to the wedding. It took her less than a minute to decide what to do about it. Bingley had charge of the day-care center now; she didn't need the money for that. The rectory was in good shape. The roof of the church was fixed and solid.

She would pay herself the ten thousand dollars' back salary that was owed to her by St. Bede's.

On Monday morning a bus would be leaving for New York City, that musician's paradise abounding with stores full of instruments and music. Mother Gray would be on the bus. On Monday evening it would return, and Mother Grey would be on it then too, carrying a decent playable cello in a good case and an armful of sheet music.

Maybe she would even get her hair done.

Match wits with the best-selling

MYSTERY WRITERS
in the business!

SUSAN DUNLAP
"Dunlap's police procedurals have the authenticity of telling detail."
—*The Washington Post Book World*

☐ AS A FAVOR	20999-4	$4.99
☐ ROGUE WAVE	21197-2	$4.99
☐ DEATH AND TAXES	21406-8	$4.99
☐ HIGHFALL	21560-9	$5.50

SARA PARETSKY
"Paretsky's name always makes the top of the list when people talk about the new female operatives." —*The New York Times Book Review*

☐ BLOOD SHOT	20420-8	$5.99
☐ BURN MARKS	20845-9	$5.99
☐ INDEMNITY ONLY	21069-0	$5.99
☐ GUARDIAN ANGEL	21399-1	$5.99
☐ KILLING ORDERS	21528-5	$5.99
☐ DEADLOCK	21332-0	$5.99
☐ TUNNEL VISION	21752-0	$6.99

SISTER CAROL ANNE O'MARIE
"Move over Miss Marple..." —*San Francisco Sunday Examiner & Chronicle*

☐ ADVENT OF DYING	10052-6	$4.99
☐ THE MISSING MADONNA	20473-9	$4.99
☐ A NOVENA FOR MURDER	16469-9	$4.99
☐ MURDER IN ORDINARY TIME	21353-3	$4.99
☐ MURDER MAKES A PILGRIMAGE	21613-3	$4.99

LINDA BARNES

☐ COYOTE	21089-5	$4.99
☐ STEEL GUITAR	21268-5	$4.99
☐ BITTER FINISH	21606-0	$4.99
☐ SNAPSHOT	21220-0	$4.99

At your local bookstore or use this handy page for ordering:

DELL READERS SERVICE, DEPT. DS
2451 South Wolf Rd., Des Plaines, IL. 60018

Please send me the above title(s). I am enclosing $ _____
(Please add $2.50 per order to cover shipping and handling.) Send check or money order—no cash or C.O.D.s please.

Dell

Ms./Mrs./Mr._____

Address _____

City/State _____ Zip _____

DGM-11/95

Prices and availability subject to change without notice. Please allow four to six weeks for delivery.

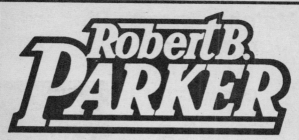